Heaven
on Earth

Heaven
on Earth

VANESSA MILLER

WHITAKER
HOUSE

HEAVEN ON EARTH
My Soul to Keep ~ Book Two

Vanessa Miller
www.vanessamiller.com

ISBN: 978-1-62911-290-9
eBook ISBN: 978-1-62911-291-6
Printed in the United States of America
© 2015 by Vanessa Miller

Whitaker House
1030 Hunt Valley Circle
New Kensington, PA 15068
www.whitakerhouse.com

Library of Congress Cataloging-in-Publication Data

Miller, Vanessa.
  Heaven on earth / Vanessa Miller.
    pages ; cm. — (My soul to keep ; Book 2)

Summary: "A rags-to-riches young man must find a way to convince his lady that true love feels so much better than all the money and career success in the world"– Provided by publisher.
  ISBN 978-1-62911-290-9 (softcover : acid-free paper) — ISBN 978-1-62911-291-6 (ebook)

1. African Americans—Fiction. 2. Self-realization in women—Fiction. 3. Self-actualization (Psychology) in women—Fiction. I. Title.
PS3613.I5623H43 2015
813'.6—dc23
                    2014045455

1 2 3 4 5 6 7 8 9 10   22 21 20 19 18 17 16 15

Prologue

One by one, everyone took a seat and sat forward, looking attentive. Tamara's father, Bishop David Davison, opened his Bible and said, "Please turn with me to Psalm fifty-one." When the pages stopped turning, he began reading, starting with the first verse:

> "Have mercy upon me, O God, according to thy lovingkindness: according unto the multitude of thy tender mercies blot out my transgressions. Wash me thoroughly from mine iniquity, and cleanse me from my sin. For I acknowledge my transgressions: and my sin is ever before me. Against thee, thee only, have I sinned, and done this evil in thy sight: that thou mightest be justified when thou speakest, and be clear when thou judgest. Behold, I was shapen in iniquity,

and in sin did my mother conceive me. Behold, thou desirest truth in the inward parts: and in the hidden part thou shalt make me to know wisdom. Purge me with hyssop, and I shall be clean: wash me, and I shall be whiter than snow. Make me to hear joy and gladness; that the bones which thou hast broken may rejoice."

When he had finished reading, her father looked out over the congregation. Tears were running down his face as he said, "For months now, you all have heard false allegations against me, and those of you who love and know me believed us when we told you that what was being said about me wasn't true. I thank you for standing by me.

"But today, I stand before you and confess that I have sinned against my family and against God. For although those allegations were false, my wife and I have hidden another secret for thirty years. It wasn't right for us to do this, and it ends today."

Sitting next to her, Solomon was holding his breath, as if he could hardly believe what his ears were hearing. On his other side, Larissa, who'd been raised along with Tamara and her siblings and was now dating Solomon, grabbed his hand and squeezed it.

"You see," Tamara's father continued, "I am not a perfect man, just a man who happens to love Jesus. But before my wife and I gave our lives to the Lord, I had an affair with another woman, resulting in the birth of a son. My wife and I were separated at the time; but, as I counsel married couples all the time, separation doesn't give you the right to go out and hook up with someone other than your spouse. I learned the hard way that what I did was wrong, and my family has been paying for my infidelity ever since. The biggest price has been paid by my son Solomon, with whom I never had a relationship because I was too ashamed to acknowledge the sinful act I had committed."

He looked down at Solomon and said, "I hope that, one day, you will be able to forgive me for what I did, Son. Because I want to be your father more than anything in this world."

Tamara had seen tears spring to Solomon's eyes when her father had called him "Son." Then Solomon had stood and stridden over to the podium. He'd put his arms around her father and cried on his shoulder. "I forgive you, Dad," he'd sobbed. "I forgive you."

It had been a touching moment. Tamara had even shed a few tears. But it hadn't been long afterward when tongues had started wagging, especially when it was revealed that her brother Adam also had a secret child.

Her close-knit family had always been known as a morally upright bunch, as pillars of the community. Tamara had been proud to be part of the Davison clan. But now she wanted no part of them anymore. In truth, she just wanted to run and hide. So, she'd done the next best thing: quit her job at her father's church and accepted a position in Atlanta, almost four hours away from her family and the craziness that now surrounded them.

It remained to be seen whether the craziness would follow her there.

1

Snapping her fingers to Marvin Gaye's "Trouble Man," Tamara Davison tried to put herself in the right frame of mind for the interview she was scheduled to do the following day with the illustrious Jonathan Hartman. The man had indeed come up hard, as the words of the song repeated over and over; but there was nothing hard about Jonathan's life these days. It made Tamara wonder if this song was still on his playlist. Uncovering the answer to that question could be the start of an awesome interview series that could lead to a gig on CNN or even Fox News, or so she hoped.

Tamara was tired of the knockoff, wannabe, so-called travel station she was working for. She wanted more—much more. So far, she had been allowed in front of the camera only a few times since being hired by the network. Most of her time was spent writing copy for the lifestyle magazine the network owned.

She needed to make a move quickly, because she couldn't let things continue the way they had been going. If only she no longer depended on the monthly checks her father sent to her, as if money could cover his guilt for having ruined her life and destroying her ability to trust men in general. Only recently had she learned the truth about the father she had long considered perfect—a man who pastored a thriving megachurch in Charlotte. Years ago, he had fathered a child out of wedlock and kept it a secret for decades. And after he'd finally welcomed his illegitimate son back into the family fold, it had gotten out that Tamara's brother, Adam, had done the same thing as his old man. She was through with both of them, and with every other member of their species.

If this interview went well, she could start earning her own living and tell her father that he could keep his money.

Looking as dapper as ever in a khaki two-button blazer, snug fitted jeans, and dark brown slip-on Prada loafers, Jonathan Hartman was all smiles as he strutted into the banquet hall where this year's All About the Future luncheon was being held. This was Jonathan's third year hosting the event, at which he gave away college scholarships to deserving high school students. But this was his first time hosting in the town where he'd grown up, in New Orleans, Louisiana. And it was the first time in years that he'd been back. Fifteen years ago, he'd left home to attend the University of North Carolina–Chapel Hill. Shortly into his junior year, he'd transferred to Howard University in D.C. After graduating, he'd taken on his first fixer-upper, and he hadn't bothered looking back. He doubted anyone would blame him.

Jonathan vividly remembered the warm summer day when he'd glanced out the window and had seen the children playing in the front yard of the run-down house across the street. He'd wanted to join them, but after countless instances of begging his mother to let him, she'd finally given him an answer.

"You can't ever play with those kids," she'd told him flatly. "Your dad wouldn't like it, and then he would stop making his child-support payments."

"Where is my dad?" Jonathan remembered asking. "Why doesn't he ever come to see me?"

His mother had opened the curtain and pointed at the very house where those kids were playing. "Your dad lives there," she'd said. "He's those kids' dad, too, and he don't want his precious wife knowing that he fathered a kid by another woman. Now do you understand why you can't go playing with them?"

The news had shaken his seven-year-old world like nothing else. So deep was the wound that his mother's revelation had inflicted on him that he'd never been able to completely heal from the pain.

When tears had started rolling down his face that day, his mother had taken him in her arms. As she'd rocked him, she'd said, "I'm sorry, Son, but I guess it's high time you knew the truth. I wish I could take back what I did to you, but if I could, you wouldn't be here. We both just have to live with it."

After the hurt Jonathan had experienced as a child, he'd never wanted to come back to this city. He felt no nostalgia for the Big Easy. Had no desire to walk through the French Quarter or sample the seafood, nor did he want to listen to any of the numerous jazz musicians posted on the street corners. Plus, his mother lived in Florida now, so it wasn't as if he'd been obligated to come back to visit her. But his business manager had informed him that they had received a petition signed by kids at three local high schools there, and Jonathan had finally agreed that he couldn't avoid this town any longer. But he'd made sure that the ballroom in which the luncheon was scheduled was on the opposite side of town from where he'd grown up.

"Mr. Hartman, thank God you're here!" his assistant, Lisa, greeted him. "You had me worried for a minute there."

Her worry was understandable—Jonathan was known for being early without fail for everything. His grandmother had been nicknamed "Early Bird" because she didn't just believe in being on time; she arrived well beforehand for everything. "The early bird gets the worm," she used to tell him. Jonathan had adopted the same behavior, and he'd gotten quite a few worms because of his grandmother's advice.

But Jonathan had delayed on purpose because he didn't plan on spending even one minute more than he had to in this town. "Everything's all set, then?

Lisa nodded. "Of course. I was just waiting on you to arrive so we could get started."

"Well, I'm here, so let's get things moving. I have a plane to catch."

She raised an eyebrow. "I thought you might want to hang around your hometown for at least a little while. Don't you have any old friends you want to see before heading back home?"

"Any friends I had here moved away a long time ago, just as I did." That was the easy response, much better than admitting that he hadn't made any lasting friends in this town. Jonathan had never felt good enough for anything or anyone until he went to college. But he hadn't kept many friends from college, either. Maybe he should change his bio, removing any reference to his birthplace. That way, no one would assume that he had any connections to this godforsaken town.

"Well, don't run off too fast, because you have an interview with Tamara Davison from the Word in Action network right after the luncheon."

He couldn't hide the smile that crept across his face—the first genuine grin he'd given since arriving here. "I won't forget. I'm looking forward to it."

Looking down at her notes, Lisa added, "Ms. Davison told me that the two of you are old acquaintances. Sounds like at least one of your former associates stuck around."

"Tamara doesn't live here. I met her in college." Jonathan wanted to tell her that he and Tamara were friends, but the way things ended between them left a big question mark on that.

As Lisa jotted something on her notepad, Jonathan walked past her and entered the banquet hall. He was caught off guard as the room exploded with applause, all the banquet attendees standing to their feet. It wasn't that this was unusual for All About the Future events—he knew that Lisa always told the award recipients to applaud as soon as he entered the room. But, in this town, where he hadn't even been allowed to speak to his own father or play with the neighbor kids, the applause didn't seem warranted. It felt as if, at any moment, everyone would figure out who he was and revoke their applause, reminding him of the nobody he used to be.

"Thank you so much for what you're doing for our kids," one of the mothers said as she approached him with outstretched hand. "My son had given up on the idea of going to college until we found out about the scholarships your organization provides for underprivileged students."

"You don't have to thank me," Jonathan said as he shook her hand. "I'm just making good on a promise I made to God back when I didn't know how I would be able to afford college. The Lord made that happen for me…and so much more."

The woman beamed. "And it's my prayer that the Lord will do the same for my son, and for the rest of these kids, as well."

"Just tell him to dream big and stay focused, and I guarantee you, he will succeed."

The woman's eyes filled with tears as she put her hand on Jonathan's shoulder. "God bless you, Mr. Hartman. You are truly heaven-sent."

"I don't know about that, but I thank you for saying so."

Soon Jonathan took his place at the table where Tamara Davison was already seated. He smiled at her, praying that she wouldn't be able to tell what he was thinking. When they were in college together, Jonathan had dreamed that Tamara was his girl, but he'd never summoned the courage to ask her out. A cheerleader, she'd dated jocks exclusively, and Jonathan had always felt that he didn't measure up. In those days, that feeling had prevailed in just about every area of his life. So, he'd kept quiet about his attraction and contented himself with just being friends.

Finally, it had reached the point where Jonathan couldn't pretend any longer. That was when everything had changed.

But they weren't in college anymore. And Tamara had traveled a great distance to interview him. Maybe these days, being successful in business rather than on the basketball court or the football field meant something to her. He was about to lean across the table to say something to her, but the emcee took his place at the podium and began his opening remarks before he could do so.

Before long, Jonathan was summoned to the stage to award the scholarship certificates. There were twenty recipients in all. Ten of them would receive a full ride for four years, five of them would enjoy a full ride for two years, and the last five would have their first year of school covered. The extent of their reward was based on three simple areas: academic performance, community service, and financial need. Jonathan had established the criteria for the scholarships, but he never got involved in deciding who would receive them.

Once the emcee handed him the certificates, he stepped up to the podium and began calling the names of the recipients of the four-year full-ride scholarships. One by one, the awardees walked onstage, accompanied by their parents or guardians, to accept their certificates and shake his hand. They wore the grins of kids who knew that life would never be the same for them.

Handing out the certificates brought tears to Jonathan's eyes. This ceremony was always bittersweet for him, because it brought back memories of how tough it had been to grow up in a single-parent household, raised by a mom who often didn't have enough money to put food on the table.

In those days, Jonathan had never imagined that he would make something of himself. He had certainly never thought he would enjoy the kinds of riches God had blessed him with. And that was the primary reason he gave back through the scholarship program. Didn't the Bible say that it was more blessed to give than to receive? Jonathan appreciated all the people who had helped him along the way. He only prayed that these kids would someday come to experience the blessings of giving because of what had been given to them.

Finally, it was time for the third group of recipients to come up to the stage—those who would receive a one-year full-ride scholarship. Most of the students in this group had earned mediocre grades and had done just enough community service to get by. So, they were receiving awards compensatory to their labor. But each year, someone in this third tier always managed to do something that surprised Jonathan. When that happened, he made sure that the scholarship money kept flowing until he or she graduated. He wondered who would be the surprise in this year's group.

When he reached the final name, he stammered. "C-carter Washington." Reeling from the thoughts running through his head, Jonathan tried to calm himself. There had to be more than one Carter Washington in the state of Louisiana.

He recalled the last time he'd seen Carter, the only kid from across the street who'd ever said a word to him. He'd been two years old; Jonathan, fourteen. He remembered the moment as if it were yesterday—Carter holding out his hands and saying, "Pick up! Pick up!" over and over to him. Jonathan had frozen. His mother had always warned him to stay away from the Washingtons, and now, there he was, with one of them asking to be picked up.

"Pick up," Carter repeated, still holding out his hands.

Pointing at himself, Jonathan asked, "You talking to me?" He shot a glance back at his house to see if his mother was looking out the window. He wasn't even supposed to be on this side of the street, but he'd wanted to pass the slow-moving grandma out for her afternoon walk on the "right" sidewalk as he made his way home from school.

Carter hugged Jonathan's leg and smiled up at him.

Jonathan couldn't help himself—he bent down and picked up the little boy. "Hi, there." His eyes locked on the gaze of his young half brother.

Before he could do any further bonding, the little boy's mother rushed outside, grabbed her son out of Jonathan's grasp, and pulled him inside the house.

The Carter Washington who stepped forward was unmistakably the same one he'd met all those years ago. As he handed him his award, Jonathan's heart thudded as he met the gaze of the man who had accompanied the young man on stage. He was staring directly into the eyes of Philip Washington, the man who'd had a hand in his birth, the man who sent child support checks but had never wanted anything to do with him.

"Thank you, sir," Carter was saying. "I've improved my grades, so I'll graduate with honors, and I'm gonna make something of myself, just like you did. I promise. I've already been accepted at UNC–Chapel Hill—your alma mater."

Jonathan wanted to say something encouraging—something that would motivate the young man to hit the books and leave the partying to the other kids. But he couldn't get his mouth to open.

"Cat got your tongue?" Philip sneered. "You can't even say hello to your little brother?" He snatched the certificate from Carter's grasp and flung it in Jonathan's face. "You've already insulted your brother by awarding him a lousy year of paid tuition, while those snot-nosed brats down over there get to enjoy a free ride for four years." He tossed his head at the previous groups as he dropped the certificate on the floor and stepped on it. "Keep it. We don't need your charity." He grabbed hold of Carter's arm. "Come on, Son. We'll find another way to get you through college."

The room fell silent; nothing was heard but the sound of Philip's boots as he stomped across the stage with Carter scurrying behind. As he passed Jonathan, Carter whispered, "Thank you."

Not knowing what else to do, Jonathan called up the last recipient and handed off her award. Then he turned off the podium mic, stepped off the stage, and left through the back door of the banquet hall.

2

He did *not* just pick up and leave without saying a word to me," Tamara fumed under her breath. She couldn't believe what had just happened.

Well, she could understand why Jonathan might be upset. If someone had just blasted her for not helping one of her brothers in a time of need, she'd be upset, too. But her family had brought so much trauma and drama to her life that Tamara doubted anyone would question her for not wanting much of anything to do with them. She didn't know what Jonathan's family had done to him; but, in truth, she didn't care. He'd had no right to dismiss her the way he had.

Jonathan's corporation was headquartered in Charlotte—the hometown of the family she'd been avoiding for the last two years. She didn't want to go back, but it was time for her to put on her big-girl pants, because Jonathan Hartman was her ticket to the big time. She'd had a pleasant childhood with plenty of wonderful experiences growing up as a Davison. However, the discovery that her dad had fathered a son that no one had known about for nearly thirty years, added to the recent news that her brother had been hiding the daughter he'd conceived outside of his marriage, had just about destroyed every happy memory.

She wanted to be as far away from her dysfunctional family as she could possibly get. But for the chance to do this interview, she might be willing to go back. Still, she refused to stay in her parents' home. She would simply book a room at the Marriott in Uptown and charge it to her company. It would be a business trip, after all—nothing personal about it.

"A room for one night?" the clerk asked when she approached the counter in the lobby.

It was late, so she wouldn't be able to look for Jonathan tonight. And tomorrow was Saturday, so it was doubtful whether she would catch him in his office. But she was confident in her abilities to track him down, even if the process took a day or two. "Check me in for two nights, to be on the safe side."

The clerk nodded, tapping away on his keyboard. Then he handed her a key card. "Enjoy your stay."

Tamara thanked him and headed for the elevator. Just then, a swarm of people came through the entry doors. Tamara was thankful that she'd beaten them to the registration desk. The last thing she wanted to do was stand in a long line, only to find out that all the available rooms had been taken by this group.

"Tamara! Tamara Davison? I can't believe it's you."

Tamara couldn't see who was calling her; she saw only a hand waving up and down from the midst of the crowd. Several moments later, a woman broke free from the group. When Tamara saw her, she wished she had checked in at another hotel. It was Belinda Wallace—the last person she wanted to see.

Still, she pasted on a smile as Belinda ran over and wrapped her arms around Tamara as if they were the best of friends, not longtime rivals. One of Tamara's fellow cheerleaders on the squad at UNC–Chapel Hill, Belinda had been responsible for Tamara's first broken heart. The entire time she'd thought the star quarterback was in love with her, he had been sneaking around behind her back with Belinda. Once Tamara had broken up with him, the two had stopped sneaking around and had gone public with their relationship. They'd gotten engaged during senior year, and Tamara assumed they were still married.

"It's been ages!" Belinda gushed as she released Tamara and stepped back. "I wondered if I would see you this weekend."

She frowned. "We haven't seen each other since college. What would make you think you might see me?"

"I've been praying for you throughout this past year, but I never had the courage to call you," Belinda admitted.

Tamara folded her arms cautiously across her chest and stepped back, as if she still needed to protect herself from Belinda. "Praying for me? That's strange, for someone who stole my boyfriend right out from under me." She realized she sounded childish, but she couldn't help it. Even though she'd stopped pining for the quarterback long ago, the sting of Belinda's betrayal still hurt.

"Can we sit down for a minute?" Belinda asked, seeming unfazed by the cool response. "I'd really like to talk to you."

Tamara wanted to reject her, just as she had rejected Tamara's friendship in favor of a cheating, no-good scoundrel. But she reminded herself that those things happened when they were both just nineteen years old. That had been ten years ago. The least she could do was hear her out.

She followed Belinda to a set of chairs in the hotel lounge. As they sat down, Tamara couldn't resist a dig. "How's Tony?"

Belinda tossed her head back with a bitter laugh that caught Tamara off guard. "We're divorced. He wasn't a very nice man. He married me because I got pregnant during our senior year of college, but he never let me forget that I was his charity case."

Tamara couldn't believe it. "I—I'm so sorry. I had no idea."

"That man makes no sense. I don't think he even understands himself." Belinda shrugged. "Let's just say that I got a lot more than I bargained for when I stole him from you."

There was a sadness in Belinda's eyes that made Tamara feel almost guilty for having carried a grudge against her for all these years.

One of the women who had entered the hotel with Belinda walked over and handed her a key card. "We're all going up to the rooms. No one wants to go out tonight, so we'll just order pizza. Is it okay if we assemble in your room for dinner?" the woman asked.

Belinda smiled. "Sure, that'll be fun. I'll be up in a little while; I just need to finish talking with an old friend of mine."

The woman greeted Tamara briefly before heading to the elevator with the other women.

Tamara turned to Belinda and raised her eyebrows. "What brings you to town, anyway?"

"Women Against Domestic Violence," Belinda answered without hesitation. "I'm the convention chairperson this year, and a lot of the members flew here with me."

Tamara didn't know what to say to that. In her wildest imagination, she never would have placed the beautiful, smart, confident woman as a victim of domestic violence.

"Believe it," Belinda said at the surprised look on Tamara's face. "As I said before, Tony was not a nice man. He abused me—physically, emotionally, and mentally—for the entire five years of our marriage. He brought me down so low that it took the love of God to lift my head again."

Before Tamara even realized what she was doing, she reached out and put her hand over Belinda's. "I'm so sorry that happened to you. I never would have thought Tony capable of doing such things."

"Me neither. For years, I imagined the wonderful life we would have together. After the birth of our daughter, Tony got drafted by the NFL and life was good…until he realized he was no longer the star on the team as he had been in college. That's when he started knocking me around."

Tamara shook her head. "Did you tell anyone what was going on?"

"Today's NFL is not like it used to be years ago. I told Tony's coach and also talked to the team owner, but neither one did anything, except to suggest that I not aggravate him, and that I pay closer attention to his mood swings. As if it was my fault that he was using me as a punching bag!"

"That's terrible," Tamara muttered.

"Not as terrible as the thoughts I used to have back then." Belinda leaned back in her seat. "I started blaming you for what I was going through."

"Me?" Tamara couldn't keep from sounding shocked.

"I know it's unreasonable…I was so filled with hate during those years. I just wanted someone else to hurt as much as I was hurting. But once I broke free from Tony and gave my life to the Lord, I realized that I had no right to wish such a horrible situation on you. I've been praying that God would send a wonderful man into your life ever since—a man who will cherish you and realize just how special you are."

Tamara was humbled by those words. The woman had come a long way from the girl she'd been in college. "Thank you for that."

"I was so excited when I found out that our convention would be in Charlotte this year. A group of us are going to stay over on Sunday to attend your father's church." Belinda opened her purse and started rummaging through it. Soon she pulled out a long white envelope. "I planned to bring this to the service on Sunday, but I guess I can give it to you now."

Tamara accepted the envelope from her. It was wrinkled and worn-looking, as if she'd been carrying it around in her purse for a long time. Stamped and addressed to the church, it bore Belinda's Chicago residence as the return address.

"I wrote this letter to you a year ago but never found the courage to mail it." Belinda stood with the hint of a smile on her face. "We were friends once, and I ruined that. But I truly hope that we can at least be friendly to each other, even if you aren't willing to salvage our friendship."

Belinda walked away, and Tamara looked at the envelope again. She was tired from her flight, and the conversation with Belinda had nearly drained the rest of her strength. All she wanted to do now was go to her room and sleep until morning. She put the envelope in her purse for later reading, and went to find her room.

As Tamara laid her head on the pillow, she was reminded of something Belinda had said. She and some of her friends would be attending Tamara's father's church on Sunday. Her father would most certainly know that she was in town once Belinda informed him that she had spoken with her. Whether she liked it or not, the nature of this trip had just become personal.

$$\backsim$$

Jonathan had a fitful night's sleep. He'd left the banquet hall and driven straight to the airport. Once home, all he'd wanted to do was close the door to his condo and shut down his mind so he wouldn't have to think about the awful scene with the guy who'd donated the specimen necessary for his conception. But he couldn't get his mind off the man—or the whiskey he'd smelled on his breath. And for the first time in his life, Jonathan wondered if his mother might not have done him the biggest favor of all by not allowing him to be raised by a man like Philip Washington.

He had been tempted to call his mother when he got home, but she was living in Florida, having the time of her life with a man she'd recently married after a few years of dating. He didn't want to take the smile off her face by bringing up bad memories from the past in the middle of the honeymoon phase of her marriage.

Consequently, Jonathan got little rest from the demons of his past. He wasn't as alert as he normally would have been the next morning when he arrived at the office. "Hey, Lisa," he groggily greeted his assistant as he passed her desk. "Give me a few minutes before starting our weekly meeting, okay?"

"I'm not Lisa, but if it will get me that interview you promised, you can call me Lisa, or even 'Hey, you,' for all I care."

Caught off guard, Jonathan turned and stumbled backward. Catching his balance, he took in the vision of loveliness seated at his assistant's desk. "Tamara?" He pressed a hand against his chest. "You might give someone a heart attack, sneaking up like that."

"I didn't sneak. Is it my fault that you need glasses? Or maybe that's the way you treat your assistants—you walk past them without as much as a 'Good morning,' just barking out orders, not even looking their way."

He raised his hands in surrender. "I wasn't trying to be rude. I just have a lot on my mind at the moment." Lowering his arms, he let out a sigh. "What can I help you with?"

Tamara stood, giving him a better view of her beautiful figure. Her hair was pulled back, and she wore a white pantsuit.

As she strutted toward him, Jonathan wondered if she knew how seductive her movements were.

"I was hoping that you would be able to speak with me this morning. I really need this interview."

Her voice was as sultry as her image was exotic. She reminded him of one of those island beauties he'd seen on travel commercials, enticing folks to vacation in the Bahamas, Jamaica, or some other place made for running barefoot on the beach.

"Um…I'm pretty busy over the next three weeks, but I'm sure we can figure out a date to reschedule. Won't you step into my office?" He gestured to the door across the hall. "Sorry about bailing on you yesterday."

"Thanks. I appreciate you making time for me."

He'd like to do a lot more than make time for this woman. When they were in college, he'd dreamed of making a life with her. But he didn't have time for pipe dreams now—not when reality was slapping him in the face.

~

Tamara needed to figure out how to play this lousy hand she'd been dealt. Jonathan was her ticket to a better job than the one she currently held at the low-budget cable network. That would mean better pay—finally, she could stop depending on her dad's handouts. She knew Jonathan was a busy man, but she had used their college friendship to get the interview. Now to think of a way to get herself on his priority list.

Crossing her legs to get comfortable on his sofa, she watched as he took off his jacket and slipped it over the back of his chair. The man was a dream in motion—biceps, triceps, and oh-my-goodness. The skinny kid from college was now eating well and obviously lifting weights, too.

"You've changed," she told him.

"I haven't really," he protested as he sat down. "I'm still the same Jon-Jon you knew in college. It's just that I have a hectic schedule these days."

"I understand. But I really need this interview. I'm at the D level in my career, and this could be just the ticket to boost me to the C level."

Jonathan smiled sympathetically. "I wish I could help, but any moment now, Lisa is going to march through that door with a long list of to-dos for me."

"I hear you, Jonathan. All I'm asking is that you add me to that list. How about I tag along with you today? We can do the interview in bits and pieces."

Before Jonathan could answer, his office phone rang. He held up a finger. "This is Lisa now." He hit the speaker button, then grinned at Tamara as he said with exaggerated friendliness, "Good morning, Lisa!"

Evidently, Lisa had no time for niceties. "Mr. Hartman, I have someone on the line who needs to speak with you. She says it's important… something about your brother."

"What brother?" Jonathan barked into the speaker.

"She says his name is Carter, and he's in some kind of trouble."

Jonathan rolled his eyes heavenward. "Put her through."

Tamara couldn't believe that he didn't turn off the speaker function to speak privately with this woman, but her inquisitive mind also wanted to know what had happened to the young man whose father had rejected the scholarship money at the banquet. So, she kept quiet and just listened.

"This is Amanda Washington," the woman began when the call was connected. "I know you don't care much for me, considering everything that happened. But this isn't about me. Carter is in trouble."

"What did he do?" Jonathan asked, as if presuming the kid's guilt.

"He didn't *do* anything. But your daddy is dead, and the police have arrested Carter as a suspect in his murder."

Jonathan jumped out of his seat, shock etching his face. "What did you say?"

"You heard right. Now, can you help Carter or not?"

Had the woman no compassion? She'd just told Jonathan that his father was dead. Tamara may not have been as close to her father as she used to be, but to hear that he was dead would destroy her.

Jonathan glanced at his watch and then looked around the room, his eyes appearing unfocused. "I...I can't leave my office right now," he finally said.

"Figures. I told Carter that you wouldn't help him. I don't know why that boy puts so much faith in you."

Her response somehow changed things for Jonathan, because he cleared his throat and said, "Let me clear some things off my calendar, and I should be able to get there in a day or two. I'll call my attorney and see if he can get Carter released on bail or something." Jonathan grabbed a pen and piece of paper. "I need your address."

"You know where we live." With that, the woman hung up.

She reminded Tamara of her brother Adam's wife, Portia—a real treat to be around. "I'm so sorry for your loss, Jonathan," she told him. "That woman had no right to speak to you that way."

He plopped back down in his chair. "I'm used to it. And it isn't as if I lost that much."

She stood from her seat and walked around to his side of the desk. "Your face tells a different story. You loved your father, didn't you?"

Jonathan almost laughed, but he kept his mouth shut as he lowered his head.

Tamara put her hand on his shoulder. "Tell me how I can help you. We were once good friends, and you could use a good friend right now. You shouldn't have to go through this alone."

Jonathan ran his hands across his face, then swiveled his chair around to face Tamara. "My attorney can get Carter out on bail, but he's no criminal defense lawyer."

"And you're wondering if I know one?" Tamara smiled as she thought of her half brother, Solomon. "Wonder no more, because I'm related to one of the best."

3

When her plane had landed in Charlotte, Tamara had harbored no intentions of attending her father's church. But after her discussions with Belinda and Jonathan, she realized there was no way she'd be able to avoid the Davison clan.

Jonathan had spent all of Saturday in meetings, which meant that the only time he was free to meet up with Solomon was Sunday. So, Tamara reluctantly agreed to let him walk her to church that morning. Not wanting to draw attention to herself, she selected a seat for them in one of the very back pews. Soon after the service began, her father was behind the pulpit, preaching like there was no tomorrow and he was duty-bound to get every soul present saved today.

Tamara was happy for him. He'd suffered a heart attack several years prior and had been bedridden for some time. Nobody had known for sure if the charismatic bishop David Davison would ever be physically strong enough to stand behind the pulpit and go as hard for the Lord as he'd done in decades past.

To make matters worse, while her father had been resigned to bed, her brother Adam had taken over all the bishop's responsibilities at the church. Adam was a skilled church administrator, and Tamara thoroughly enjoyed his preaching style. The problem, however, was that his evil wife, Portia, felt entitled to more than she was due. She'd even plotted to take the church, and everything that David Davison had spent twenty years building, for her own greedy pleasures. Thankfully, Portia's scheme hadn't played out; but, for Tamara, it had been the last straw—the event that had compelled her to distance herself from the rest of the Davisons.

She returned her attention to her father, who was now reading from the fifteenth chapter of John's gospel:

"I am the true vine, and my Father is the husbandman. Every branch in me that beareth not fruit he taketh away: and every branch that beareth fruit, he purgeth it, that it may bring forth more fruit. Now ye are clean through the word which I have spoken unto you. Abide in me, and I in you. As the branch cannot bear fruit of itself, except it abide in the vine; no more can ye, except ye abide in me."

Although she remained calm on the outside, Tamara was shaken to the core by that Scripture. She hadn't been doing much "abiding in God" as of late. She had been living in Atlanta for a year now, and she hadn't even attempted to find a church to attend on a regular basis. Her father had given her a list of churches to check out once she got settled, but she hadn't visited even one of them.

Her daddy's presence was so powerful that he didn't have to be speaking directly to her in order to get a point across. She closed her eyes, trying to block out her need for a family, even one that had let her down. A family that hadn't quite lived up to the gospel that was preached here every Sunday.

"Listen closely to the Scriptures," her father exhorted the congregation, "because many of you think you've got this Christian thing all figured out, simply because you attend church every Sunday and would never even consider missing a midweek service. But I'm here to tell you that God wants far more than that.

"In this wicked world in which we live, all Christians must ask themselves whether they are a fruit-bearing branch on the Vine, or if they've dried up and are about to fall away." He placed a hand on his pulpit Bible as he looked out at the congregation. "You see, going to church is a good thing. It's the place where we come to get charged up so we can go out into the world and make a difference by advancing the kingdom of God into every sphere of society." He pointed toward the doors at the back of the sanctuary that opened to the outside. "It's your responsibility, as Christians, to always have a ready word for a hurting nation—a nation that has turned its back on God.

"But here's the good news…some people look out at this nation and feel that it is so full of sin and that Christians no longer have a place here. But my Bible tells me that where sin does abound, grace does much more abound. So, this is no time to slack off. Rather, we need to become bolder in our zeal and tell whosoever will listen to us that it's not too late, that the love of God is long and strong enough to meet every man just where he is."

Listening to the preached Word of God, Tamara realized how right her father was. If no one had been there to tell Belinda about the love of God when she was going through the painful aftermath of a broken marriage, what would have happened to her? Belinda was clearly a different woman from the backstabbing, boyfriend-stealing one she'd been in college. It was more obvious to Tamara now than ever before that the world needed God—that He really made a difference in people's lives. And she found herself face-to-face with her own need for God.

Tamara wasn't sure if her dad had seen her, since she was seated in the rear of the sanctuary, but when the service had concluded and he'd given the benediction, he stepped down from the pulpit, whispered something in her mother's ear, and then strode toward the back of the church, beaming. As he neared her, he opened his arms. "My baby has come home," he boomed. "Thank You, Lord Jesus, my baby has come home!"

Tamara stood and made her way toward her father. Unexpected tears filled her eyes as she allowed him to hug her. She couldn't move far enough away to escape the fact that she had once been Daddy's little girl—and probably would always be, at least to a certain extent.

As the congregants made their way out of the sanctuary, Tamara overheard some of them whispering about how she had left the church and wondering, loudly, if she had repented and decided to come back. As far as Tamara was concerned, they should have been asking those questions about her brother and his crazy wife. She found herself almost regretting coming to church, but the warmth of her father's embrace quickly dispelled those thoughts. No amount of gossip or glances of disapproval could take away how loved she felt in this moment.

A longtime friend of Tamara's ran over and gave her a hug. "Tam-Tam! Why on earth didn't you tell me you were going to be in town?"

Tamara felt a stab of guilt. She had neglected her family and friends for two years, and the only reason she'd come back was because she'd needed a favor. "I'm sorry, Erin. I should have called."

"I'm afraid it's partly my fault," Jonathan said as he came over and joined them. "I've been keeping her busy this weekend."

Tamara turned to him. Part of her wanted to thank him for giving her an excuse, but she didn't want her father misinterpreting what he meant by "keeping her busy." Putting a hand on Jonathan's shoulder, she turned back to her father. "Daddy, this is Jonathan Hartman, a friend of mine from UNC. He's been gracious enough to allow me to tag along and interview him for a piece I'm working on."

Her father extended his hand to Jonathan. "Nice to meet you. And thank you for coming to church with my daughter this morning."

Erin grabbed hold of Jonathan's other hand. "Jonathan Hartman… of Hartman Enterprises? The company responsible for constructing that new shopping mall on the south side of town?"

Jonathan smiled. "Yes, that's my company."

"Ya don't say." Erin was gripping his hand as if she planned never to let go.

Tamara pried her friend's fingers away and muttered, "I'll call you later. We can talk then."

"You'd better call me," Erin demanded, staring pointedly at Jonathan. Then she whispered in Tamara's ear, "Girl, this one's better than some baller. His money's not contract-based."

Erin had a long history with "ballers." First she'd dated a Hornets basketball player, until his contract had run out. Then she'd fallen in love with a Panthers linebacker. But that linebacker had recently been in the news because of certain legal troubles—troubles that threatened to cost him his very lucrative contract. Tamara wouldn't be surprised if the beautiful but flawed Erin Luell was already in the market for her next high-profile, high-paycheck man.

"Very powerful message you delivered today, sir," Jonathan said to Bishop Davison. "It gave me a lot to reflect on."

The bishop beamed. "I'm glad to hear it." He turned to Tamara. "Why don't the two of you hang out with me in my office while your mom finishes her meeting with the women's ministry?"

"Sure thing, Dad," she told him, then said good-bye to Erin.

As they headed for the side door of the sanctuary, she spotted Belinda with a group of ladies from the convention. Her first inclination was to keep walking, pretending not to have seen her. But then she remembered Belinda's comment about wanting to at least be friendly if they couldn't be friends.

"Hey, Belinda." She waved to the woman as she and her friends made their way down the aisle. "I see you made it to church."

"And I'm so glad I did. I'd heard about how dynamic your father was, not just as a preacher but also as a teacher of the gospel. And, I must say, I was impressed. Too bad I live in Chicago."

"I'm sure you have plenty of excellent preachers there, as well."

Belinda nodded. "I am happy at the church I attend." Her eyes darted behind Tamara.

She turned to see Jonathan waiting patiently behind her, so she introduced the two, hoping that Belinda wouldn't fawn all over Jonathan, as Erin had.

A strange look appeared in Belinda's eyes as she studied Jonathan, and Tamara thought, *Here it comes.*

But Belinda merely turned back to Tamara, gave her a hug, and said, "It was nice seeing you this weekend."

That was it. The woman hadn't made any attempt to find out more about Jonathan. Once again, Tamara was impressed by the progress Belinda had made in her life, especially in terms of her character, while Tamara herself had been standing still.

She led Jonathan to her father's office, and they had just sat down when Solomon walked in. Thank goodness. She could get down to business and get out of there. She hugged her half brother. "You're just the man I was looking for."

"Oh, yeah? You wanted to tell me you love me, huh? Is that the reason you called yesterday?" Solomon teased.

"If you had answered your phone yesterday, you would know. I mean, seriously, Solomon—what kind of big brother ignores a call from his youngest sister?" Tamara chided him.

"His cell phone's broken—the third one this year," said Larissa, Solomon's wife, as she stepped into the office. She gave Tamara a hug. "It's so good to see you! You should come home more often. Aunt Alma has really been missing you."

Tamara dearly missed her mother, too; she just didn't know if she wanted to be at one with her family at this point in her life. So, she focused her attention on making introductions.

"It's good to meet you," Jonathan said as he shook Solomon's hand. "Tamara speaks so highly of you."

Solomon grinned. "She'd better."

Tamara was about to retort when she noticed her mother standing in the doorway, looking straight at her, as if she were a prodigal who'd finally returned home after a ten-year absence.

"Don't just stand there, Alma," Tamara's father told his wife. "Come on in here with the rest of us."

"I was just making sure I wasn't hallucinating," Tamara's mother told him as she walked over and wrapped her daughter in her arms.

Tamara felt her eyes pool with tears once more, just as when her father had hugged her. How could someone love two people so dearly yet, at the same time, not want to be around them? Life could be so complicated.

"I have missed you so much, Tamara. You're only a few hours down the road. You really should come home more often."

"I will, Mama. I promise."

"You'd better mean it. Because I would hate to embarrass you on that job of yours, but if you don't start coming home more, I'm calling your boss and complaining about all the work he's piling on you. No one should have to work so many weekends. It's not fair to you or your family."

Tamara sighed. "I'm not a kid anymore, Mama. You can't just call my company and tell them to lighten my workload."

"I wouldn't test her if I were you," her dad said with a wink.

"Daddy! You can't let her do something like that."

"Tell you what," her father said. "Come home today and have dinner with the family, and I'll see if I can control your mother's urges to embarrass you on your job."

Tamara chewed her lip. "I'm not sure I can make dinner. I brought Jonathan here so he could speak with Solomon."

"We're all headed back to Dad's house for dinner," Solomon told her. "Come with us, and we can talk there."

Tamara wanted to scream at him. She didn't want to be in that house—the place where she'd grown up and made so many wonderful memories…and others that were not so wonderful. But instead, she smiled sweetly and said, "In that case, how could I miss Sunday dinner?"

"You can't tell me the Lord doesn't answer prayers," her mother said as she slung her purse over her shoulder.

Jonathan drove Tamara to her parents' house, following her directions. "How long has it been since you last saw your parents?" he asked her en route.

Tamara rolled her eyes heavenward. "I haven't been home in a little over a year, but I talk to them all the time. My mother was just being a drama queen."

Jonathan gave her a wide-eyed glance. "If I went an entire year without showing my face at my mother's, she'd send the coast guard after me."

Tamara wasn't amused. She didn't need anyone else making her feel guilty. She had her family for that.

4

Alma Davison gave a regal welcome to as many of her children as wanted to come for dinner after church every Sunday. Today, everybody but her firstborn, Adam, was in attendance. He and Portia were still battling over his acceptance of Britney, a child he'd fathered with another woman while engaged to Portia. According to Tamara's sister, Leah, the family rarely saw Adam these days as he struggled to repair his crumbling marriage.

As Tamara stood in the kitchen with her mother, Leah, and Larissa, helping to plate the meal, Tamara realized how much she'd missed this weekly tradition.

Leah glanced up from her spot at the kitchen island, where she was working on carving the roast chicken. "What's wrong, Mama?"

Alma shook her head as she dumped the steamed green beans into a serving bowl. "I guess I'm just dumbfounded. I don't understand why Tamara waited so long to come home. And it wasn't even to see her family—it was to conduct an interview for work."

Tamara groaned. "I'm sorry, Mama. It's just that I've been really busy. I can't be in two places at once."

"I realize that all of you are grown now, and you have your own lives, but your daddy and I brought you into this world, so we deserve to see your face every once in a while," her mother admonished her.

Larissa pulled the dinner rolls out of the oven. "You didn't bring me into this world, Aunt Alma, but you've always been a mother to me. You know that Solomon and I will always come home to visit."

Alma pulled Larissa into a sideways hug. "You've always been a blessing to me. I'm the luckiest woman in the world because I have children whose births didn't require me to endure nine long months of pregnancy and eight-plus hours of hard labor."

That comment stung. Even though she'd been the last child born to Alma Davison, she'd also been the most difficult—and she'd never been allowed to forget it. Tamara truly loved being around her mother; things had just gotten so complicated. She wished that she could explain her reasons for moving away, but it would only cause her mother distress and guilt, and Tamara didn't want that. So, she decided to try to make light of the situation. Planting her hands on her hips, she said, "I'm glad the two of you are so close. Now maybe you can just write me out of the picture altogether."

"We wouldn't dream of doing such a thing," her mother assured her she wrapped her other arm around Tamara. Soon Larissa and Leah had closed in for a group hug. "We love you too much."

"Okay, okay," Tamara giggled. "I believe you. Now, can we eat before I pass out from hunger?"

The women stepped back, giving Tamara some space. "Okay, girls, let's get this food on the table," her mother said. "I'm sure our men are hungry, too."

"Speaking of men..." Leah nudged Tamara. "When did you hook up with Jonathan?"

"I didn't 'hook up' with him. I'm doing an interview on him, and that's it. Strictly business."

Smirking, Leah teased, "If you say so."

"I say so. Please drop it."

But Leah wasn't ready to drop the subject. The moment they carried the dishes of food to the dining room and set them on the table, she turned to their guest. "So, Jonathan, do you live in Charlotte now? Or did you fly here with my sister?"

Tamara just shook her head. Leah was too nosy for her own good.

"I relocated my company here about two years ago," Jonathan said as they all sat down for dinner. "The expansion of the business district has kept us busy."

"Are you in real estate or construction?" Solomon asked as he helped Larissa into her seat.

"I do both. In the beginning, I bought and sold fixer-uppers to individuals looking for a decent home at an affordable price. These days, I'm more on the commercial property end of things."

Leah gave Tamara a gentle kick under the table. "And you're not married yet, right?"

Jonathan laughed. "No, I've been way too busy building my business these last few years. But I'm hoping to settle down one of these days."

"What church do you attend, son?" Tamara's father chimed in.

"I live in the southwest part of town, so I've been attending several churches on that end. But nothing has felt like home just yet," Jonathan replied.

"Well, you're more than welcome to come back to the Worship Center of God," Alma told him as she beamed at her husband from across the table. "I can personally vouch for the bishop of that church. He is a true man of God."

"You don't have to sell me on that point," Jonathan told her. "After hearing his message today, I was already planning on returning."

Tamara wanted all of this chitchat to come to an end. How dare they recruit Jonathan to attend their church before his bottom had even warmed his seat? *Give the man a break*, she wanted to scream. "Daddy, will you please bless the food so we can eat already?"

"Sure, baby girl."

All heads were bowed and eyes were closed as Bishop Davison thanked the Lord for the food and for every person around the huge table. After the "Amen," he looked around and said, "It's always good to break bread with our family and friends. Thank you all for coming. Now, let's eat!"

After dinner, Solomon took Jonathan to the bishop's office so they could discuss the situation with Carter. Meanwhile, Leah grabbed Tamara by the arm and pulled her in the direction of the back patio, Larissa following.

"What's this all about?" Tamara wanted to know. "Jonathan and I should be leaving soon."

Larissa closed the patio door behind them. "We haven't seen you forever. Before you sneak out of here, we need to have some sister talk."

"I'm not 'sneaking out' anywhere," Tamara protested. "I happen to live in Atlanta. So I can't be around my family every waking moment of my life anymore."

"Not that you want to be around us." Leah eyed her sister. "I think you're ashamed of your own family."

Who wouldn't be ashamed of them? Tamara wanted to say. After all, her own sister had tried to extort money from their father when she had found out about his secret son.

But Tamara didn't want to bring up sour memories. She finger-combed her hair and rolled her eyes. "Whatever."

"Keep on being flippant, and you won't be promoted to godmother anytime soon," Larissa said as she placed her hand over her abdomen.

Tamara arched an eyebrow at Larissa. "Are you trying to tell me something?"

"Of course she is, silly!" Leah was practically jumping up and down. "Larissa's pregnant!"

Tamara was elated for Larissa, but she was surprised to see her sister so happy for her, too. Ever since Larissa had moved in with the family when she was a teenager, Leah had been in competition with her, feeling threatened by Larissa's beauty and intelligence. Had Leah softened? Tamara would have loved to have been around to see whatever it was that had brought about her apparent change of heart.

And being that she was most likely the last to learn the wonderful news about Larissa and Solomon, Tamara was beginning to think that staying away from home for so long might not have been the smartest decision she'd ever made.

"Well, say something, girl!" Larissa demanded.

"I'm sorry…I'm just at a loss for words. I guess I never thought that I would miss so much, living just four hours away. Now you're getting ready to have a baby." Tamara reached out and hugged her sister-in-law. "Congratulations, girl. I'm really happy for you and Solomon."

"I'm going to fight you for that godmother job," Leah joked.

Ignoring her, Tamara asked Larissa, "When did you find out? When is the baby due? What do you want, girl or boy?" She wanted to know all the details at once.

Larissa graciously answered each of her questions in satisfying detail. After a while, she said, "Enough about me and the baby. Tell us the truth about you and Jonathan."

"I keep telling you, there's nothing going on. We're here together on business, nothing more."

"You've got to admit that it looks suspect," Leah said. "You and Jonathan were inseparable in college."

"We were good friends our freshman and sophomore years, but then he transferred, and I never heard from him after that."

"And now you're *back together again*," Larissa said with a grin.

"You two are very funny. But all I'm interested in is an interview."

Leah rolled her eyes. "Come on, Tamara. You can't tell me you haven't noticed how good Jonathan looks. I remember him from your college days. The boy was so skinny I wondered if he knew where the cafeteria was. But he ain't skinny no more." She paused for a high five with Larissa before she added, "Being wealthy is one thing; being wealthy, handsome, and buff ought to be a sin."

"Then maybe you should date him, because I'm interested only in the interview."

Larissa shook her head. "At one time, you were the social butterfly around here. You had more dates than Leah or I could have dreamed of. But now, all of a sudden, you don't hang out with your friends, and you don't date. What gives?"

Tamara shrugged. "Things change...people change."

"They don't change that much, Tamara. What is so wrong about the idea of sharing your life with a man who makes you happy?" Larissa asked her.

"Marriage and kids are what the two of you want. But I'm not wired that way. I would sooner curl up with my pillow and the knowledge that my heart is safe and intact than waste time cultivating some relationship that's doomed to fail from day one."

Shaking a finger at her, Leah said, "Oh ye of little faith. How can you just count yourself out like that?"

Less than an hour later, Tamara was back in Jonathan's car, heading for her hotel. Her parents had tried to convince her to spend the night with them, but she'd used the excuse that she'd left all her things at the hotel.

"Thanks for introducing me to your brother," Jonathan said as they drove along. "Solomon seems very capable of handling Carter's case."

"He should be. Solomon specialized in criminal law when he lived in LA, before he was burned by a guilty client he managed to get acquitted. If Solomon takes the case, it'll be because he believes your brother is innocent."

"He is innocent. Carter would never kill his own father."

Tamara turned and studied Jonathan for a moment. "I never knew that you had a brother. And I'd thought that you and I had talked about everything in college."

He raised one shoulder, then lowered it. "Some things are too painful to talk about. You were always going on and on about your father, his ministry, how wonderful he was… I just couldn't bring myself to tell you about my situation."

"You could have, you know. Then I would have toned down the gushing a little."

"I probably need to recline on a couch and pay someone to listen to my problems." Jonathan was smiling, but it didn't sound like he was joking.

"I'm here. You can talk to me for free."

Jonathan's hands were locked on the steering wheel, his eyes focused intently on the road ahead. "Is this Tamara the reporter asking? Or Tamara, the girl who used to be a good friend?"

"A little of both, I guess. It's kind of hard to turn off the reporter in me. But I will try my best to listen without grilling you like a reporter. How's that?"

Jonathan sighed as he pulled into the parking lot of her hotel. He drove up to the door and stopped the car. "You'd better get some sleep. We leave first thing in the morning."

Tamara stared at him. "You're taking me with you?"

"Do you still want the interview?"

"I…I do, of course. I just didn't think you'd have time for me, with everything you've got going on."

"You'll have my complete attention on the plane ride, I can promise you that."

"Well, in that case, just tell me what airline, and I'll be there."

"United. The flight leaves at nine in the morning."

"Okay. I'll go online and try to book a seat on that plane."

Jonathan was almost laughing. "I don't think you understand. I already had my assistant order your plane ticket. You'll be flying first class with me."

"Oh." She was surprised that he would purchase a ticket for her without first making sure she was willing to go with him. But then, she figured that he hadn't become as successful as he was by asking for permission.

"I hope you don't mind. You did follow me back to Charlotte to get an interview, so I figured you wouldn't want to go home without it."

He had a point. "That was thoughtful of you." She opened the car door and hopped out. Before she shut it behind her, she said, "I'll meet you at the airport in the morning."

"I can pick you up, you know."

"That's okay, but thanks. I'll just meet you there." Tamara shut the door and ran inside before he could convince her otherwise.

5

Tamara was excited to have an opportunity to travel with Jonathan, but something in the way he'd handled the whole situation made her uneasy. Was he trying to tell her something? She hoped that he wasn't interested in hooking up with her, because that certainly wasn't happening.

As she started packing her suitcase so she'd be ready to go first thing in the morning, her nerves got the better of her. She plopped down on the bed, picked up her cell phone, and called Larissa.

"What's going on, girl?" Larissa asked.

"I don't know what to do. I need your advice."

"Of course, I think you should move back home. Do you want me to come to Atlanta to help you pack up?" Larissa was joking, but not really.

"I'm not calling about moving home. Jonathan wants me to fly to New Orleans with him. He claims he's going to allow me to interview him on this trip. But I'm worried that he might have other things on his mind."

"Other things…like what?"

"Like, maybe he wants to date me or something."

Larissa laughed. "You make it sound like a date with a millionaire is the worst thing that could happen to you. Why don't you just relax and let things unfold as they may?"

"Haven't you been listening to me? I don't won't anything to develop between me and Jonathan…and it's not just him I'm talking about. I don't want anything to develop with anyone. Ever."

Larissa made a sound as if she was about to make a comment, but then thought better of it. Finally, she said, "Look, Tamara. I know you. You're not about to pass up an opportunity that will help to advance your career. So, go on the trip, and I'll tell Solomon to watch out for you."

Tamara wanted to object to that. She wasn't a baby. She didn't need her big brother policing her. But then, she thought about how handsome Jonathan was. It wasn't just his fine appearance—he'd been a looker back in college, too. It was that now, he had an air about him that he hadn't had before. Confidence virtually oozed out of the man's pores, and Tamara was afraid that she might get caught up in the slime that was sure to follow. He was a man, wasn't he? That fact alone meant that trouble would follow him. And the trouble Tamara worried about most was the beautiful, bold, buxom kind that seemed to make men like her father and her brother lose their minds and forget that they had wives whom they promised to love, honor, and cherish.

"I guess I could fly back home the moment the interview is over," Tamara reasoned aloud.

"Do me a favor, Tamara," Larissa said. "Try to have some fun."

⌒

The next morning, Tamara threw on a paisley print V-neck caftan with a V-shaped hemline. The fabric of the knee-length dress had gold and purple swirls and Tamara felt like an African princess whenever she wore it. Plus, it was comfortable—an essential quality of one's clothes while traveling. Looking nice didn't hurt, either. Sometimes it got a woman through security and other airport lines faster.

Tamara caught a cab to the airport, where the driver stopped by the United Airlines terminal. Once he had lifted her bags out of the trunk, she gave him a tip, then looped her tote bag over the handle of her suitcase and wheeled her luggage into the airport.

She stood just inside the doors, looking left and right for any sign of Jonathan. Soon someone hollered her name, but he didn't sound like Jonathan.

"Tamara," the man said again, closer this time.

She turned and plastered a smile on her face at the sight of Eric Jordan. She'd gone out with him a few times before finally realizing she was making a serious mistake. Just like all the other jocks she knew, Eric was a serious player. "Hey, Eric. How've you been doing?"

Eric shook his head. "Not so good. I've been waiting on a certain lady to return my call." He checked his watch, then met her gaze again. "For about a year now."

She sighed. "I've been really busy. My career keeps me on the move."

"How long does a phone call take?" Eric gave her a nudge. "I was hoping we could hang out…you know, like we used to."

"I'm sorry, Eric, but with my current schedule, I just don't see how I can manage a relationship."

"Look, I get it—you want your freedom. No rules. No labels. I can flow with that. Just give me a call."

She placed her hand on his shoulder and gave him a pitying look. "Eric, listen…you're a really nice guy, but—"

"Come on, honey." Jonathan kissed Tamara on the forehead as he slid his arm around her waist. "We'll miss our flight if we don't get going."

Tamara gazed up at him as if he were her knight in shining armor, come to her rescue. At that moment, she wanted to thank him by wrapping her arms around his broad back and planting a lingering kiss on his perfectly luscious lips. But she didn't want to start anything that she couldn't finish, so she quickly came to her scenes. "Hey, *honey*. I've been looking for you."

"Is that right?" Jonathan asked, beaming from ear to ear.

Eric frowned. "Who's this?"

Jonathan extended his hand. "Jonathan Hartman."

"Eric Jordan" came the wary response. Still eyeing Jonathan dubiously, Eric muttered to Tamara, "I thought you didn't have time for a relationship."

"Nice meeting you, Eric," Jonathan cut in. "We've got to go catch our plane." He started ushering Tamara away, toward the check-in counter.

As they hustled off, Tamara whispered, "I know what you're thinking."

"What?" Jonathan said, his eyebrows raised innocently. "I'm just glad you made it here on time."

"You were worried I wouldn't?"

He gave her a wry smile as he relieved her of her luggage. "Well, you were late for class just about every other day when we were in college."

She dropped her jaw for a moment in a show of mock indignation. Then she shrugged. "My hair was a lot longer back then. It took me at least an hour to get it just right."

He cast her a glance, then nodded approvingly. "I like the new look. That bob suits you."

She patted her auburn hair. "Thank you, sir."

"So, I heard some news regarding your family."

Tamara came to a sudden stop. "Who said something about my family?"

"Calm down." Jonathan held up a hand. "I thought Larissa's pregnancy was a positive thing. But if you don't want to talk about it…."

Tamara had almost stopped breathing as she waited for Jonathan to explain what he meant. Even though her father and brother had done wrong, she still couldn't bear the thought of gossips murmuring about them.

Smiling to cover up her initial reaction, she said, "Of course it's good news. I can't wait to spoil that baby."

"What will you be, an auntie or the godmother?"

Tamara thought about that for a moment. She was fairly certain how it would play out. "They're pretending that I'm in the running for godmother, but Larissa will most likely pick Leah for that role. I'll probably be the godmother to Leah's baby, whenever she gets married and has one."

"Does that mean Larissa is out of the godmother business until you settle down and have a baby?"

She groaned. "Don't you start that crazy talk, too. How many times do I have to say that I am happy with my career and don't need anything else to fulfill me? I'm a woman with a plan that does not include a man and a bunch of babies."

"Really?" Jonathan sounded genuinely surprised. "I never thought of you as a career-above-all-else kind of woman."

She knew why he was shocked. When they were in college and Tamara was dating Tony Wallace—the quarterback everyone had known would go pro—she'd told him that she wouldn't mind being a homemaker while her husband served as the family's financial provider. That model had worked for her mother and father, and back then, she'd seen no reason why it wouldn't work for her, too. But that was then. A lot had changed.

"Well then, change the way you think of me." Tamara went to grab her luggage back from him. "I've got it."

"I don't mind," Jonathan said, keeping his grip on the suitcase as he continued toward the check-in desk.

Normally, Tamara would have protested his taking of her suitcase as if she were some helpless female who couldn't walk a few steps without begging for the help of some big, strong man. But Eric was still watching them, and she didn't want to spoil the image Jonathan had so skillfully created of them as a couple. With a brief wave good-bye to Eric, she rushed to catch up with Jonathan.

She reached him just as he was retrieving their tickets from the kiosk. Then he took a luggage tag and prepared to tie it around the handle of her suitcase.

"I can do it," Tamara insisted, snatching the tag from his hand.

After completing the task, she glanced at Jonathan and saw that he was chuckling at her. She refused to ask what was so funny. If he wanted to act like a laughing hyena, who was she to stop him?

He pointed at the tag. "I didn't have a chance to write your name on it. And you'll probably want to include your address, as well." He handed her a pen.

"Good thinking." She bent down and filled out the tag with her contact information, trying to ignore his ongoing laughter. But she couldn't help it—she was annoyed. When she straightened, she told him, "So what if I like to do things myself? Is that such a crime? A single girl's used to taking care of herself."

Nodding toward the airport entrance, Jonathan said, "Eric what's-his-name would love to do anything and everything you ask, I'm sure. The man looked positively love struck when I arrived."

She removed her tote bag from her suitcase, which she then handed over to be checked and stowed beneath the plane. "Just a case of a man not being able to take no for an answer."

"Is that right?" Jonathan asked as he turned in his own bag, then started in the direction of the security checkpoint.

"Sure is." Tamara fell into step beside him.

"He looked like your type. I don't know why you'd tell him no in the first place."

She pointed at him. "I *knew* you were thinking it."

He shook his head. "Was not."

"You don't fool me one bit, Jonathan Hartman. In college, you were always on my case about dating jocks. You said that only gold-digging women wasted their time with…what did you call them?" She snapped her fingers, trying to recall the exact phrase he used to say. "Lunkheads! That's what you always called the jocks."

He chuckled. "Well, that was then. For your information, I no longer think of jocks as 'lunkheads.' Many of them go on to become talented businessmen once their professional careers come to an end."

"But you do still believe that only gold-digging women chase after those kind of men?"

"I don't think you're a gold digger, Tamara. Your family always had money, so you never needed to worry about finding a wealthy man to marry."

As they joined the line of passengers waiting to pass through security, Tamara told him, "I have plenty of friends who want to strike it rich by marrying a pro-baller. I'm just not into that kind of thing anymore."

"All grown up and breaking hearts, huh?"

She shook her head. "The last thing I want to do is break anyone's heart. But I am fully focused on making a success of my career. So, I really don't have time to think about dating anyone."

"And you don't think you can have a successful career *and* a man?" Jonathan inquired.

Tamara shook her head. "One would be a distraction from the other."

"See, that just goes to show how much I know. Because I'd always thought that having success in business and in love would be the best of both worlds."

What Jonathan considered the best of both worlds, Tamara considered torture, not to mention that it posed a high risk of causing her downfall. Lately, she'd given up the idea of dating a man even with no strings attached, no expectations for the future. She was committed to her career, and she wasn't about to let anyone cause her to lose sight of that.

But she could admit, at least to herself, that seeing Larissa so happy about her pregnancy had done something to her. In her hotel room the night before, as she'd lain all alone after her phone conversation with her sister-in-law, Tamara had found herself wondering if she was making the right decisions with her life. One thing kept her on the path she'd chosen, and that was the broken heart she was sure would result the very moment she let down her guard.

A man who couldn't be faithful to his family shouldn't have one. Tamara didn't know if any man could be faithful. And she wasn't about to risk her own heart to find out.

Their conversation was suspended as they made their way through security, the taking off of shoes and belts and stepping through metal detectors always proving a hectic process.

"What are you thinking about?" Jonathan asked once they had boarded the plane and were seated next to each other, waiting for takeoff.

"Huh? Oh, nothing."

"It doesn't look like 'nothing.' Your eyes are like this"—he scrunched his eyelids till she could barely see his pupils—"so I know you're thinking about something pretty serious. Fess up, Tamara. If you were thinking about me, just admit it."

She leaned back against the headrest and looked at him. "Are you just being nosy, or do you really want to know my thoughts?"

"It seemed like you were thinking about something important. But if it's too personal, I don't want to pry."

"I'm the one who's supposed to be prying into your business, remember? I'm here to interview you."

"I feel you," Jonathan said as he leaned in closer to Tamara. "But it's been so long since I've seen you. You can't just interview me without telling me what's new in your life, too."

Tamara smiled at Jonathan. She didn't know how or when it had happened, but she felt comfortable with him again. Just like she'd felt in college, when they would spend hours upon hours together, studying, watching movies, and just hanging out. Letting loose, she said, "Okay, so what do you want to know about me?"

6

What did he want to know about Ms. Tamara Davison? Only everything and then some. He tapped his forefinger against his chin. "Let's see. What do I want to know?" He angled his body toward her, then let his eyes trail slowly down the length of her body, stopping at her shapely legs. She wore a knee-length dress, but when she was seated, it exposed her muscular thighs. "Are you a runner now?"

Tamara followed his gaze. "I prefer to use the EFX machine and to do a bit of fast walking. Running is bad on the knees." She held out her hand to him. "Now may I please borrow your jacket?"

Chuckling, he took off his blazer and draped it over her lap. With a smirk, he said, "If you don't want anyone admiring your legs, you may need to start wearing full-length dresses."

"Or maybe you should stop leering at me," she suggested as she positioned his jacket so that it completely covered her legs.

"Woman, you wound me." Jonathan made an exaggerated wince as he brought his hands to his heart. "'Leering' makes me sound like a dirty old man. I was simply appreciating what's in front of me."

"Okay, well, ease up on the appreciation. I'm here on business. That's it."

"Of course you're here on business. I invited you," Jonathan affirmed. "But I'm the one asking the questions right now. So, tell me, Ms. Tamara Davison, why aren't you married with three kids by now? I know you said that your career is your top priority, but I still think you have motherhood on your mind."

"Why aren't you?" Tamara asked, throwing his question back at him.

Jonathan wagged his index finger at her. "Oh, no. Your interview hasn't started yet. It's my turn, remember?"

She rolled her eyes. "Whatever."

"You didn't answer my question."

She eyed him head-on and said firmly, "I don't want to be married. There, does that answer your question?"

Actually, it didn't. "The Tamara I used to know wanted nothing more than to marry the man of her dreams and have a bunch of kids. So now I'm left wondering what man was responsible for destroying your dreams." Jonathan was smiling as he posed the question, but one look at the expression on her face made his grin disappear. He held up a hand. "I didn't mean to upset you. Just forget that I asked. It's none of my business, anyway."

Still scowling, Tamara said, "Not every woman dreams of having a husband and kids, you know. Some are more career focused, like me."

"And that's your prerogative. I shouldn't have pried."

The tension subsided from her face as she let him off the hook. "You didn't do anything wrong. I guess I just get tired of everyone expecting me to have a plus one. I just wish people could understand that I enjoy my own company and don't need a man to validate me."

Jonathan leaned back in his seat. "I admire your self-confidence. I've been single and career focused for so many years that, lately, I've begun to wonder if I chose the right path."

Tamara's brow furrowed. "How can you say that? You'll probably be voted most successful at your high school and college reunions. I remember how...well, how tight money was for you all those years ago." She put a hand on his arm. "No offense, but you did work two jobs and were signed up for the two-meal-a-day plan instead of the three-meal plan almost everyone else had."

"And you used to bring me peanut butter crackers so I wouldn't go hungry." He grinned at the memory.

She nudged him with her elbow. "I had to. You were so skinny, I thought you were going to fall out of your clothes, walking all over campus."

Jonathan patted his stomach. "Well, I'm not skinny anymore." He wasn't fat, by any means; he'd just developed muscles over the years and bulked up to be the six foot two, two-hundred-pound specimen he now was.

"That's what I'm talking about. Suppose you had been looking for love all these years rather than building a business? You might have gotten yourself a wife and a few kids by now, but I doubt you'd be as successful. Could you live with the knowledge that you threw your potential away for something that's just going to end in heartbreak?"

"Since when were you such a cynic?" he asked, eyeing her in disbelief.

She shrugged. "I'm a realist. You've just been too busy building an empire to take note of what's really going on in the world these days, but I'm here to tell you that people don't keep their word. They might claim to be in love with you one minute, but don't turn your back, or they'll be running around on you, making you look like a fool."

"You sound as if you speak from experience." Jonathan was fascinated. In college, Tamara had been so optimistic about the future, so hopeful about marrying the man of her dreams. Now she just seemed bitter.

Tamara's gaze drifted away from him and out the window. "Let's change the subject."

So, he did, and they struck upon a conversation about adventures. Tamara seemed to be enjoying herself as she told him about the many places she'd traveled over the last two years, most of them for her job as a reporter. When she rattled off the various natural disasters that she'd covered, Jonathan told her about his trip to Haiti in 2010 following Hurricane Katrina to help with the cleanup efforts.

"Shut up! You went to Haiti?" Tamara was becoming more animated, and she leaned toward him, evidently eager to hear more.

He nodded. "I also helped out in New Jersey after Hurricane Sandy."

"I think that's fantastic. So many people are willing to help another country through times of hardship, but when it comes to their own nation, they just sit back and wait for others to step up to the plate."

"Have you been following the ice-bucket challenge?"

"Of course. I even did it myself a few weeks back." Running her hand through her hair, Tamara proudly said, "Got my head wet and everything. But it was for a good cause. My prayer is that they'll discover a cure for ALS as soon as possible."

"Mine, too," Jonathan said. "But what I couldn't understand was the number of Americans who became so offended because, as they said, we were dumping cold water over our heads—in the name of a good cause, mind you—while there are thousands of children in Africa in need of fresh water. As if it was a sin to 'waste' a bucket of water in the interest of raising money for people in need in our own country."

"Those comments were so silly," Tamara agreed. "It wasn't as if we could have shipped that water overseas, anyway."

"Thank you. My thoughts completely." Jonathan shook his head. "I say, let's find a way to help in any way we can, in a way that's appropriate for the given cause."

Tamara studied him with a pensive look. "You know, your eyes light up when you talk about helping others. Is that why you began your scholarship program?"

He shook his head. "It wasn't because of the rewarding feeling I get from helping others, even though that's a valid experience. It was because I truly believe what the Bible says: *'For unto whomsoever much is given, of him shall be much required.'*" With a shrug of his shoulders, he added, "I don't think I'd be able to look myself in the mirror if I didn't do as much as I possibly could to help others in need."

"Why is it so important to you?" Tamara prodded him, making him suspect that her interview was now under way.

He just grinned at her.

"Come on, spill it," she insisted.

"You won't believe me."

"Try me," she said, looking even more intrigued.

"Okay, here goes." He took a deep breath. "There are two reasons why I believe in giving back. God is one, and the other is…you."

"Me?" Tamara's eyebrows went up. "What did I do?"

"God first, and then I'll get to you. When I was a kid, things were pretty tough; there were times when my mom didn't have enough money to buy even a measly loaf of bread. I remember crying out to God one night. I prayed that He would make me successful so that I wouldn't have to go hungry. And I promised Him that if He would take care of me, I would lighten His load by reaching out and helping others."

He turned and looked Tamara in the eye as he continued. "By the time I started college, I had pretty much forgotten the promise I'd made to God. But there you were, helping out at the homeless shelters and volunteering your time tutoring students who were struggling. One day, I asked you why you did those things, and I never forgot what you said." Putting his hand on his hip, Jonathan tried to mimic the sound of Tamara's voice: "My father says that people receive a greater blessing by giving than by taking all the time."

Tamara laughed. "I don't talk like that." She sobered as she confirmed, "My father always said that to us when we were young, and I believed him. I used to believe every word that came out of the good bishop's mouth."

"And now?"

She shrugged. "Now I'm older, and wise enough to realize that no one is right all the time."

"Well, I'm here to tell you that you were right back in college. Your words changed my life. I have been blessed to earn a very good living, but I feel even more blessed when I'm giving to others. So, thanks for sharing some of your father's wisdom with me."

"It's actually biblical wisdom, as you know. The Bible says, 'It is more blessed to give than to receive.' My father was just paraphrasing the Scriptures, as he often does."

Jonathan nodded. "Growing up, I never had anyone around who could speak godly wisdom into my life. I'm sure your father's influence helped to make you into the wonderful, dynamic woman you've become."

Her eyes moistened as she laid her hand on his arm. "You really think I'm dynamic?"

"I wouldn't have said it if I didn't."

She blinked away her tears. "Thanks, Jonathan. These last few years, I haven't felt all that dynamic. But I've made up my mind to make some things happen in my life."

Their eyes met, and he held her gaze. But then she turned away, released his arm, and leaned back in her seat, placing her hands primly in her lap.

∽

Tamara didn't understand what was happening to her. She had just been gazing into Jonathan's eyes, imagining that she was his and he was hers. She'd thought she meant it when she'd told Larissa that she wasn't attracted to him in a romantic kind of way. But he was just so handsome, kind, magnanimous, and...and she was losing it. The man was winning her over without even trying.

Maybe she should have stayed at home. Then she wouldn't be on this airplane with Jonathan, discovering how great a man he had become. It was so good of him to think of others when he didn't have to. And to know that her lifestyle in college had left a lasting impression on someone so accomplished made her feel validated. All through her college years, she had tried to let her light shine, and her efforts had evidently paid off. Her father would be proud. The only problem was, she wasn't so proud of her father these days. She knew that her loss of faith in him had also harmed her relationship with her heavenly Father, but she didn't know how to get back to the place of peace she'd once known in Christ.

By the time they arrived at the JW Marriott in the French Quarter of New Orleans, Tamara was so thrown off her game by thoughts of her father's failures and Jonathan's triumphs that she had to get away for some time alone.

Jonathan looked at his watch. "I'm meeting Solomon at one this afternoon, so I'm free for about an hour and a half. Do you want to grab lunch somewhere?"

"Um, thanks, but I need a little rest. I think I'll just go to my room and lie down for a while."

"Okay…well then, how about dinner when I'm done with my business today?"

She remained quiet, having no ready excuse.

"Come on, Tamara. You have to eat, and there's still that interview you need to get done."

"Okay, I'll meet you for dinner," she told him before escaping to her room. Jonathan was getting to her, and she had to take her mind off this fabulous man for at least a few minutes. Any woman would be lucky to have him in her life. She sighed at the thought as she turned on her laptop.

After checking her e-mail and responding to a few messages, she spent half an hour fiddling around in her room, then found she was getting hungry. Too stubborn to call Jonathan, she ordered room service.

While eating her ham sandwich, she perused the list of local attractions featured in the hotel directory.

Soon she was taking a ride by a horse-drawn carriage through the French Quarter, gazing about her in awe at the old-world architecture. Once the driver let her out on Bourbon Street, she walked one block over to check out the art galleries on Royal Street.

She found herself fascinated with the eye-pleasing mix of classy antique shops, boutiques, jewelry stores, and art galleries. She was happy enough to see all the shops, but it was the intricate wrought-iron balconies, many of them dating back to the eighteenth and nineteenth centuries, that took her breath away. She passed sculptured fountains and colorful gardens, all before setting foot inside her first art gallery. The overall environment was absolutely stunning and Tamara enjoyed every minute of her afternoon stroll. She had been having the time of her life and hadn't even thought about Jonathan, so she rewarded herself with the purchase of a few beignets, which she carried back to the hotel to enjoy with a fresh cup of coffee.

As she strode into the lobby, she found herself smiling at the realization that this was her first time staying in the Marriott's topmost hotel. Her company would never agree to put her up someplace this expensive. She could have been interviewing the President himself, and they still would have told her to find a cheap place to crash. But Jonathan had flown her here and made sure she had a comfortable room without looking for anything in return.

Heading to the elevator, Tamara stomped her foot when she realized she'd been thinking about Jonathan again, about how wonderful he was. "Stop that," she told herself, then wondered if she ought to throw away her deep-fried treats. After all, she had purchased them as a reward for not thinking about Jonathan.

She pressed the button to call the elevator, then stepped back to wait for the doors to open. Behind her, a woman was chewing out a bellhop for dropping her Louis Vuitton luggage. He kept apologizing, but the woman was not to be appeased. Soon she stormed off in search of the young man's manager.

When the elevator door opened, Tamara turned around and handed her bag of beignets to the hapless bellhop. "I think you deserve these," she said, then got on the elevator.

7

What do you think, Solomon? Did he do it or not?"

Jonathan was seated across from Solomon at a table in one of the hotel's conference rooms. Carter was waiting in the lobby to see him, but Jonathan had wanted to speak with Solomon first. He figured that Carter's mom was saying all sorts of hateful things about him, since he hadn't gone to her house to check on Carter. But Jonathan thought he was doing pretty good by getting on a plane and landing in the same city. Baby steps were what he needed to take right now.

"He says he didn't."

"But you talked to him. Did you get a sense for whether he was telling the truth?"

Solomon nodded. "I believe him. But let me tell you a bit about me. A few years ago, I defended a client whose innocence I would have attested to by swearing on a stack of Bibles. And on the day that we won the case, he came right out and told me that he had, in fact, committed the crime."

"That must've been awful," Jonathan said.

"It was. So much so that I even doubted my own father when it came time to defend him against some false charges. My dad was innocent, but I'm still trying to convince myself to believe in the possibility of innocence. Therefore, it might be better for you to speak with your brother and determine the matter for yourself."

Jonathan let out a long sigh. "I don't know Carter all that well, so I doubt if I could figure it out any better than you."

"You two have the same father but different mothers, correct?"

Jonathan nodded. "My so-called father lived across the street from the house where I grew up, but he never came over to say hello or to give me the time of day."

Solomon put a hand on Jonathan's shoulder. "It sounds like we have a lot in common. I don't know if Tamara told you our story or not, but I didn't have a relationship with my father until I was thirty years old. He had this whole other family, and there was no place for me in it."

"I wondered about that. In college, Tamara talked about her family all the time. I didn't recall a brother named Solomon. And then, all of a sudden, she shows up with a new brother."

Solomon laughed. "It does sound a little weird when you put it like that. But since you seemed to have lived through the same thing I experienced, I'm sure it's not too weird or confusing to you."

"I wish it were, but no, it's not confusing at all." Jonathan couldn't keep the bitterness out of his tone.

"I'm going to give you a free piece of advice, my friend." Solomon stood up and put his hat on his head. "Don't live your life bitter, and don't hold a dead man's family hostage."

Jonathan shook his hand. "I'll keep that in mind." He wanted to ask Solomon how he'd gotten over being abandoned by his father. From what he could see, Solomon and Bishop Davison appeared to have a great deal of affection for each other.

Jonathan would never get the chance to build any kind of relationship with his father. But, in truth, he doubted that he would have made much of an effort toward something like that—especially after the way Philip had treated him at the scholarship banquet.

The man was hateful and mean. Jonathan would have wanted nothing to do with him, and he could almost see how Carter might have gotten angry enough to kill a man like that. Given the way he'd disowned Jonathan throughout his life, Jonathan doubted the man had won many "father of the year" awards from his other children.

But he wanted to think positively. Of all the children who lived in the forbidden house across the street, Carter had been the only one to reach out to him. And Jonathan couldn't believe that a boy with the patient, loving eyes Carter had possessed as a child could now be guilty of killing someone.

Jonathan had managed to avoid this city and the people in it for a decade, but he couldn't ignore what would always be a part of him—not when his brother's life was on the line. He made up his mind right then and there to do whatever it took to help Carter. He'd made a vow to God that he would use his wealth to help others, and he wasn't about to turn his back on his own flesh and blood.

Just then, the conference room door opened. Jonathan turned around as Carter stepped inside. "Thank you so much for arranging bail for me," he said. "My mom wouldn't have been able to swing it without your help."

Jonathan nodded, but it took him a moment to find his voice. "How are you doing?"

"Truthfully? Not so good." Carter stuffed his hands inside the pockets of his jeans. "I was looking forward to going to college and getting out of here, the way you did. I never imagined I could get out of here until my dad told me how you had."

"I wasn't aware that your father talked about me to you." Jonathan was astonished that a man who'd refused to as much as look at him when he was a kid had known or cared what he'd been up to all these years.

"I didn't know anything about you until about six months ago," Carter confessed. "Dad heard about the scholarships you were giving out to some of the kids around here. He came home with the paperwork and told me that I was going to college."

Jonathan was starting to feel a bit more comfortable with his younger brother. He leaned against the windowsill, studying him. "You hadn't planned on going to college?"

With a sardonic smile, Carter said, "Why do you think my grades were so bad? I worked night and day to pull up my grade point average once I found out about the scholarship. That's why I couldn't do the community service you required. But Dad told me that it wouldn't matter. He said"—he stuck out his chest, mimicking his father—"'My name alone makes you a shoo-in for that scholarship money. You just focus on getting them grades up.'"

Jonathan walked over to the table and took his seat again, then pointed at another chair. "Have a seat." Carter did, and then Jonathan told him, "What your father didn't realize was that I'm not the one who reviews the applications and decides on the scholarship recipients. A panel of judges uses a checklist of established criteria to select the awardees and the particular scholarship each will receive. That means you earned the scholarship on your own—not because of your dad's name."

Carter beamed. "That means a lot—thanks. And I don't think my dad was really angry at you...more at the situation. He knew that I would never be able to finish my college education unless I had a scholarship to cover every year. And he was set on seeing at least one of his kids making it in this world."

Jonathan wanted to inform Carter that one of Philip Washington's kids *had* make it in this world, but Solomon's admonition not to hold a dead man's family hostage came to mind. He knew that he couldn't go around blaming God, Carter, Carter's siblings, or anyone else for what his father had done to him. Carter was his own person, and Jonathan wouldn't allow the bitterness he felt toward his father to get in the way of his budding relationship with his half brother.

Jonathan chose not to be insulted that Carter hadn't included him in his mention of Philip Washington's kids. They had more pressing matters to deal with, anyway.

"I know you discussed this with Solomon," he began, "but I have to ask: Why do the police suspect you of killing your father?"

Rolling his eyes heavenward, Carter said, "They claim some witness saw me running from his garage. But all I did was run next door to get help. I tried to explain that to the police, but they didn't want to hear it. They think that I'm just like my brothers, but I'm not. I've never been like them. All I ever wanted to do was make my dad proud…give him a reason to hold his head up in this town."

Jonathan could understand that desire. From the time he was old enough to understand the circumstances of his birth, all he'd ever wanted to do was give his mother a reason to hold her head high. But that was a story for another day. Right now, he needed to figure out what was really going on. "You have three brothers, right?"

Carter shook his head. "Only two now. Shawn, the oldest, got killed while trying to hold up a bank when I was ten."

Jonathan remembered Shawn from school. He'd been one year older and had played on the football team. Jonathan remembered seeing him dressed in his football jersey and wishing that he had even one athletic bone in his body, because then he could have been on the football team, too. And then his father would have watched both his sons play ball. But playing ball hadn't helped Shawn—not if he'd become the "stick 'em up" kind. Maybe that was why Philip had desired a different route for his younger son.

"My other two brothers are worse than Shawn, they just haven't gotten shot yet. But both of them are serving ten-year prison sentences for gang-related crimes."

Jonathan was getting a clear picture of how Carter's future would look if things didn't change—and quick. "I guess I can see why your father was so upset with me. He wanted to get you out of here."

"Daddy was really excited that you were coming to town. A few weeks back, he told me that I was finally going to see that he had a son who was good for something besides committing crimes. He told me that I needed to get to know you, so I could grow up to be somebody."

The bitterness in Jonathan's heart clashed with a strange feeling of something akin to gratification. His father had acknowledged his success, even if it was only for the sake of propelling a son he hadn't disowned to become like the one he had. *Lord, help me to forgive* was Jonathan's silent prayer.

Taking a deep sigh, he looked at his brother. "You can succeed, and you will, if I have anything to say about it. Your father may be gone now, but you still have a mother who loves you. And I'm going to help you make her proud."

By the time Jonathan parted ways with Carter, he was plumb worn out, so he went back to his room to take a nap. He awoke to the ringing of the hotel telephone. He reached over and picked it up. "Hello?" he answered, his voice thick and groggy.

"I thought you were going to take me to dinner."

Jonathan sat straight up and glanced at the clock on the nightstand. It was already eight thirty. "Tamara, I'm so sorry. I guess that flight tired me out more than I realized."

"Don't worry about it. I was just teasing you, anyway. I went to dinner with Solomon, and now I'm getting ready to go for a swim. After that, I was hoping to get that interview you promised me."

❧

Seconds after she ended the call with Jonathan, Tamara's cell phone rang. It was Leah. With swimsuit in hand, she answered, "Hey, chickie. I haven't heard from you all day. You must be working too hard, as usual."

"Not too hard. I just left the office."

"Do you know what time it is?" Tamara demanded.

"Hey, any day I don't sleep at the office is a good day," Leah said with a laugh.

"Whatever. You need to get a life, Sis. That job requires way too much of your time."

"It doesn't *require* it; I give the extra time because I want to excel. But I didn't call to talk about me. How are things going with Mr. Gorgeous?"

"'Mr. Gorgeous,' as you call him, just blew off a dinner invitation he extended to me. The best I can hope for is to get this interview done by tomorrow and go back home."

"I'm sorry to hear that. I was hoping that the two of you would finally get together after all these years."

Shaking her head, Tamara said, "I don't know where you even came up with that idea. It's not as if Jonathan and I were ever romantically involved. We were good friends—once. End of story." They had shared one kiss, too, but Leah didn't need to know that.

"You can't tell me you never noticed the way Jonathan always looked at you. And the two of you were practically joined at the hip every time I visited you on campus."

"Jonathan was never interested in me in that way, Leah. You're just imagining things. Just like you did back in college, when you accused me of living with Jonathan and threatened to tell Daddy."

"That's because I honestly thought you two were living together! The boy was always over at your place."

"Just to study and to hang out," Tamara explained. She wanted to shout it from the rooftop or do whatever was necessary to convince her skeptical sister.

"I get it, I really do," Leah said. "I realize now that the affection was one-sided. Poor Jonathan. He never had a chance back then, not with the way you and your friends chased after every football player in sight."

"Well, I'm not chasing after any man now. Men can't be trusted, and I don't need that kind of aggravation in my life." She switched the phone from one hand to the other, then said, "I need to go down to the pool and swim a few laps before I change my mind about exercising."

"All right, girl. I'll talk to you later. But you need to take the same advice you gave me and get a life!"

Finally dressed in her two-piece royal blue swimsuit, Tamara wrapped herself in the white terry-cloth hotel robe and headed downstairs to the outdoor saltwater pool. To her delight, the area was deserted, so she got right in the water and began to swim, relishing the solitude. She was on her third lap when there was a loud splash at the other end of the pool. Someone else had jumped in the water.

Tamara kept her head down, her strokes strong. When she reached the wall, she lifted her head, propped her elbow on the edge of the cement, and wiped the water from her eyes. Then she turned around to see a dark form making for her like an underwater torpedo. He was a strong swimmer, for sure, and as she was beginning to wonder whether she should jump out of the pool to avoid a collision, he came to a stop and stood up.

"Jonathan!" she gasped as she watched him wipe the water from his face.

"You were expecting someone else?" Without waiting for a response, he took a few steps toward her, then bent his head down and brought his lips gently to hers.

Was this really happening? His lips felt so good that she couldn't help but put her arms around him and pull him closer. She opened her mouth and hungrily kissed him back.

Leaning into her, Jonathan kissed her eyelids, her forehead, her cheeks. He placed another soft kiss on her mouth and then said, in a husky voice, "This is even better than the first time. I should have kissed you back a long time ago."

Her eyes popped open. What had she done? She pushed him away and jumped out of the pool. "I'm done swimming."

"Don't go," Jonathan called after her. "I was just beginning to enjoy myself."

With her hands on her hips, she turned back to face him. "You were enjoying yourself a bit too much. And I'll appreciate it if you don't let it happen again." With that, she spun around and left the pool area with as much dignity as she could muster.

8

Tamara ran back to her room and hid there for the rest of the evening. How could she have allowed Jonathan to kiss her like that? And why would he try to compromise her in such a manner? She was here on business, not to be played with as a toy for his enjoyment. She was used to men thinking they could do whatever they wanted with women, because they thought they ruled the world. But Jonathan was different—or so she'd thought. He'd never done anything like that before.

Oh, it wasn't that they had never kissed. But she had been the one to kiss him. She had been suffering from a broken heart, and Jonathan had been there for her. She'd taken advantage of his friendship and tried to use him to soothe her pain. The very next day, she'd realized that she'd made a mistake and acted selfishly. So, she had apologized for the kiss and moved on to another jock…only to have her heart broken again.

Tamara grabbed her cell phone from the nightstand. Her fingers hovered over the screen as she contemplated calling Leah. But if she told her sister what had just happened, Leah would only say that she'd been right all along. Not wanting her sister to draw erroneous conclusions, Tamara put down the phone and picked up her suitcase. Atlanta had the world's busiest airport; surely, she wouldn't have any trouble find-ing a flight home at the last second. Tomorrow morning, she would tell Jonathan that she was flying back home and that she would call him at his convenience to conduct a phone interview. Problem solved.

Even so, as far as Tamara was concerned, she had a fitful night's sleep. Nothing seemed right. She was confused. Between tossing and turning and waking up several times, she found herself wondering if Leah had been right about Jonathan's long-standing attraction to her. Had he hung around her so much in college because he'd had feelings for her that went deeper than friendship? What would Jonathan have done if she hadn't apologized for kissing him all those years ago?

What had he said after kissing her that evening? Something about how he should have kissed her back. Had he been referring to the time she'd kissed him in college? Maybe he hadn't wanted an apology. That kiss had happened so long ago that Tamara couldn't remember all the details surrounding it. And Jonathan had transferred to a differ-ent school not long thereafter, so she'd never had a chance to get a full understanding of the matter.

But Tamara was now firmly convinced that she didn't understand men at all. The ones she thought were loyal and true really weren't, and those she considered just friends were actually impostors waiting for the right moment to pounce on her.

She awoke at seven, unsure as to when she'd finally drifted off. The last time she remembered seeing on the clock was four. She shoved the covers off her, shuffled out of bed, and got in the shower. Afterward, feeling refreshed and energized, she put on a sundress and a pair of sandals. She was about to head downstairs for breakfast when a knock sounded at her door.

"Room service."

"Um…I didn't order anything," Tamara responded.

"I ordered it for you," said a voice she recognized as Jonathan's. "Please open the door, Tamara. I owe you an apology."

That he did. She flung the door open, put a hand on her hip, and glared at him, ignoring the bellhop standing beside him holding a tray of covered dishes. "I don't have time for breakfast. I have a plane to catch."

"Come on, Tamara. You came here to interview me. Don't let my foolish behavior stop you from doing your job."

"Should I just leave this in your room, ma'am?" the bellhop asked.

Still holding the door, Tamara thought about it for a minute. She'd been about to go downstairs to get breakfast, anyway. No reason to be childish and stubborn. Plus, the food smelled good.

"That would be nice. Thank you." She opened the door wider. "Please leave it on the balcony table."

As the bellhop left, Jonathan tipped him, then stepped into the room and closed the door. "Do you mind if I sit with you? I'd really like to explain myself."

Tamara figured the least she could do was hear him out. "Okay." They sat down at the patio table, and Tamara lifted the lid off one of the plates. At the sight of the stack of tantalizing pancakes beneath it, she couldn't help but smile. "You remembered."

Jonathan grinned. "How could I forget? When the most beautiful girl in school gorges on pancakes with strawberries and powdered sugar without fretting over fat and calories, it kind of leaves a lasting impression."

"That was when I was nineteen, with a metabolism that worked in overdrive. I'm almost thirty now, and there's no way I'm going to eat all six pancakes stacked on this plate."

"I was kind of hoping that you'd share with me."

"You got it." Tamara loaded the overturned lid with three of the luscious-looking pancakes, then handed it to Jonathan. "I can handle the rest." She picked up her fork and knife, closed her eyes for a silent prayer, and then dug in.

"You should see your face. You look like you're about to perform surgery on those poor flapjacks." Jonathan chuckled. "You haven't changed a bit."

After taking her first bite and savoring the taste for a moment, Tamara told him, "Oh, I've changed. And you need to understand something about me. I am not looking for a relationship with any man at this point in my life. I thought I made that more than clear in our conversations yesterday."

"Your career is very important to you. I get it."

Tamara lifted a hand while she chewed and swallowed another bite of her delicious pancakes. "My career isn't the only reason I don't want to date. But I don't want to discuss it right now. So, let's just say that I'm unavailable. Indefinitely unavailable." She took another forkful of pancake and pointed it at Jonathan. "You'd better hope you haven't gotten me back on a pancake kick. I haven't had these in over a year because I can't afford to gain another pound."

"Please, Tamara. You look fantastic. You could stand to gain some weight, even."

"Too bad you aren't the producer for the Chicago network I've been interviewing with."

"Chicago? Would you really move so far away from your family?"

"Why do you sound so surprised about that?"

He shrugged. "You just always seemed so close with your parents and siblings. To tell you the truth, I was surprised that you took a job in Atlanta. I kept expecting to run into you at the mall or when I was out to eat."

"By the time you relocated your business to Charlotte, I had all my things packed and was scheduled to move within the month."

"That explains it," Jonathan said, as if he'd just found the missing piece to a puzzle.

"Explains what?"

"I sent you a postcard when I moved there, but it came back marked 'Return to Sender.' I almost contacted your parents, but I wasn't sure if I should or not."

"I wasn't hiding from anyone. I just forgot to have my mail forwarded."

He looked as if his feelings had been hurt, so she added, "I'm sorry that I didn't receive the postcard. And I'm sorry that we lost contact for so many years."

"Just think—if I hadn't kissed you last night, we could have picked up where we left off and become best friends again."

He sounded as if he was just kidding around, but there was something else underlining his words, so Tamara had to ask, "Why *did* you kiss me last night?"

"You really don't know, do you?" His every word resounded with pain.

After that kiss, Tamara could pretty much guess what was on his mind, but she wasn't going to say it for him. She wiped her mouth with her napkin, then placed it on top of her empty plate and waited for Jonathan to explain.

"I think I fell in love with you about a week after we met. Probably the same day you brought me that sandwich so I wouldn't go hungry. You were so caring and compassionate, not to mention completely gorgeous, that I couldn't help but fall for you." He gave her a wry smile, then added, "But you were so hung up on Tony Wallace, the all-American football star, that you barely noticed how I felt about you."

Tamara frowned. "It isn't fair to put it like that. Tony seemed like a nice guy…he just didn't understand the concept of monogamy. I thought that I was going to marry him. But after talking with the woman who stole him from me, I'm so glad I didn't. It turns out that I was all wrong about him."

"I had hoped that once you realized Tony wasn't the man for you, you'd see that you and I were perfect for each other. Instead, you decided to go a different route."

She knew he was referring to Mike Barnes, another football player. Another dumb mistake on her part.

Jonathan's voice was forceful as he added, "I think we could have built a good life together. But you weren't interested then, and you clearly aren't interested now. I get that, and I'm not tripping. I didn't come to your room to try to persuade you otherwise. I just wanted to explain why I kissed you last night."

"I'm listening," she said, but her mind was still stuck on his comment that they could have built a good life together. That was all Tamara had ever wanted—to have something good, something real, with the man she fell in love with. But how could she hope for that now? Even if she let Jonathan into her heart, she would only make his life miserable because she would never be able to trust him.

"After meeting with my half brother yesterday, I was feeling like the kid I used to be. The one who sat by the front window, gazing across the street at the house where his father lived. Do you know that I never once saw the inside of that house?"

Tamara put her hand over his. She couldn't empathize with his pain because her father had always been there for her, but her half brother had known the same kind of pain. And it broke Tamara's heart all the more for Solomon as she witnessed the pain in Jonathan's eyes. "Things like that should never happen to kids. Parents never stop to think about the harm they might be doing to their kids," she said.

"No, they don't. But when I saw you in the pool and thought about how close we used to be—how you somehow managed to make me forget about being that little boy in the window—all I wanted to do was to be close to you. I'm not sorry I kissed you, because that moment meant everything to me. But I am sorry that I upset you. And I promise that I won't take advantage of you again. Just stay here with me a few days. Please. I really don't won't to be in this city without a friend."

Could she trust him? Tamara didn't know the answer to that question, but she did know that she and Jonathan had once been great friends. She knew that, in college, she would have done anything for Jonathan. Why should she allow a decade apart to change that fact?

She squeezed his hand tight. "You've got me for another two days, just as we planned. I can understand why you wouldn't want to be in the city all alone."

"See what I mean?" Jonathan beamed at her. "There's that caring, compassionate side of you from college. There's the Tamara Davison I know and love."

9

Immediately after breakfast, Jonathan sat down for an interview with Tamara. Right off the bat, she hit him with this: "So, tell me, Jonathan, what gives you such desperation to build this empire of yours?"

"I wouldn't call it 'desperation.' More like the desire to fulfill a long-time dream."

"But you've moved at lightning speed—in ten years, you got your company off the ground and grew it to rival many of the most respected residential and commercial builders out there."

Humbled, he smiled. "Thank you for saying that." He had hoped that the interview would focus more on his commercial properties, which were the primary projects he worked on today. He had left residential construction several years ago. But Tamara evidently wanted to go back to his early days.

"It isn't often that I talk about my days with residential building," he confessed, turning his face away. "It's not a pretty picture."

"Why wouldn't you want to talk about it? I mean, you made it, Jonathan. People want to know how it all began."

He kept his eyes averted, stalling for time, in hopes that she would change the direction of the conversation.

Finally, she said, "At least tell me about the first house you flipped."

Aggravated, he met her gaze. "See, this is why I don't do interviews. Nobody wants to hear about the mistake I made in buying a house full of mold, rats, and a roach infestation."

Tamara giggled. "Are you serious? The first house you bought had that many problems?"

"It was a disaster. First off, I barely got the loan for twenty grand to buy the dump. I was using my meager savings to repair everything in that broken-down house. Every night when I went home, I wanted to curl up in a ball and cry." He made a fist and pounded his chest. "But I'm a man, and men don't cry."

She chuckled, then sobered. "How many nights did you spend fretting over the thought of losing your shirt on your first project?"

He pointed at the digital recorder. "This has to be off the record if you want the truth."

Tamara rolled her eyes. "You are being such a baby about this. No one is going to think less of you because you had an emotional breakdown. We women actually find those liberating, so we make sure to have at least one a month."

"Very funny. Do you want the truth or not?"

Shaking her head, Tamara turned off the recorder. "Spill it, crybaby."

"It happened one night after a day of scrubbing away mold and replacing drywall, capturing rodents, and emptying several cans of Raid all through the house—I probably should have gotten my lungs checked out."

"I was just thinking the same thing. When was the last time you saw a doctor?"

"Don't worry—once the money started rolling in, I got myself thoroughly examined. I'm healthy and intend to live till at least ninety."

"Well then, I'll be coming to your funeral, because I'm going to live to be a hundred."

"It's a date," Jonathan said, grinning at her.

"We have plenty of years before I have to find a black dress for the occasion. Why don't we get back to your emotional breakdown?"

He nodded. "It happened like this: I was standing in the kitchen, feeling as if I just might survive this venture, when the pipes burst and water starting gushing out. It was the plumber's fault, and he fixed everything without charging extra, but I was worn out from the experience. I lay down that night and cried into my pillow. When I woke up the next morning, I reminded myself that God was still in control. I had prayed to Him about many different situations in my life, and He had always made a way. So, I told myself that He was still on the throne, and that I needed to get up again and push forward."

Tamara stared at him, speechless.

"What?"

She reached out and gave his arm a gentle punch. "That story should have been recorded. Why won't you let me write about it? Readers would benefit so much from seeing the man in the making, especially in a situation that would show them that it's possible to get back up after falling and succeed."

"Okay, I'll tell you what. You can write all of it, except the part about how I cried into my pillow."

"Can I say something like, 'A tear trickled down his face as he witnessed all that he had worked for going down the drain, along with the water gushing from the broken pipes,' or something like that?"

"That's good. Put it like that."

She shook her head again as she jotted a few things down on her notepad. "I don't know what I'm going to do with you."

"I know one thing you could do."

Tamara glanced up from her writing. "What's that?"

"Have dinner with me tonight. I'm supposed to meet with Carter and his mom, and I think things would go a lot better if I had a friend along."

Tamara didn't think she liked Carter's mother all that much. She hadn't forgotten the way the woman had spoken to Jonathan the day she'd called in need of help. "I guess I could come along. I don't think you should have to deal with that woman on your own. No one should suffer that much abuse without a shoulder to cry on. What time is dinner?"

"I told them I'd pick them up at six o'clock and take them to the restaurant, so could you be ready to leave by five thirty?"

"Sounds good. Just don't forget about me again, okay?"

Tamara was glad she had agreed to come along for dinner because Amanda Washington was in rare form, belittling Jonathan one minute, then demanding favors the next minute. Not to mention the fact that Jonathan had offered to take her anywhere she wanted to eat, and the woman had demanded Mexican food—in a town that was famous for its seafood.

Generous guy that he was, Jonathan took them to a four-star Mexican restaurant. As they were being seated, Amanda said, "This place might charge you an arm and a leg, but that don't mean the food is worth more than a quarter."

Carter leaned over and whispered in her ear, "Ma, please don't be rude."

"I'm not being rude," Amanda barked, loud enough for the patrons seated at the surrounding tables to hear. "You can get all excited because your rich brother takes you to a fancy restaurant, but where you gonna be when this dinner is over? Back in the ghetto, that's where."

Jonathan put a hand on Carter's shoulder. "It's okay. Let's all just sit down and enjoy our meal."

Tamara wished that she could write about this outing in her article, to highlight how Jonathan had the patience of Job. If it was up to her, Amanda Washington would have already been put in her place.

When their server brought their menus, Tamara told him, "I don't need one, thanks. I'll have a beef burrito with refried beans and rice." What else would she order but her favorite Mexican dish?

Jonathan followed suit, ordering the same thing. Carter asked for a chicken quesadilla. But Ms. Amanda went to town, ordering a taco salad, a beef burrito, and a chicken quesadilla. When she caught the looks that Tamara and Carter were sending her, she said, "What? If I don't eat it all, I'll just take the rest home. It's not like Jonathan can't afford it."

"We don't doubt that Jonathan can afford it," Tamara interjected, unable to hold her tongue any longer. "We just wonder whether you need all that food."

"Now who's being rude?" Amanda asked, giving her a pointed stare.

After the server left them, Jonathan said, "Mrs. Washington, Carter and I wanted to take you to dinner so we could discuss his case."

"Then why is *she* here?" Amanda asked, glaring at Tamara.

Tamara put a hand on Jonathan's arm. "I'm with him—you know, the one who is paying for this expensive meal that can't be worth more than a quarter."

Jonathan put a hand over Tamara's as he addressed Amanda. "I'm glad you were able to join us tonight, because Solomon believes that we have a good chance of getting the charges dropped against Carter. He has a private detective on the case right now, but we think that if someone saw Carter run out of your husband's automobile shop, then someone might also have seen the real killer when he left."

"I wanted to talk to you about this so-called lawyer you hired," Amanda started in. "I know Johnnie Cochran is dead, but couldn't you find somebody else on that dream team? Your brother's life is on the line, and you go and hire the first attorney you find in the Yellow Pages. It just don't seem right."

Jonathan squeezed Tamara's hand. She got the message—he needed her here for moral support, not to tell this woman off. So, she held her tongue. But it was hard, especially since Amanda was now demeaning her own brother.

"Solomon Harris is a well-respected attorney," Jonathan told her, speaking in a cool, calm voice. "But if you don't think he's good enough, you are welcome to find someone else."

Carter shook his head. "I don't want anyone else. I like Mr. Harris, and I trust you, Jonathan. If you say he can get me out of this jam, then I believe it."

Amanda turned her venom on her son. "You believed every word that came out of your daddy's mouth, too, and where'd that get you? I'm trying to look out for your best interests by getting you a better lawyer, and you sit here and say that you're gonna stick with the one I don't want?"

"Yes, that's what I'm saying," Carter told her. "The only reason you're making a fuss about it is because of your resentment toward Jonathan. But I don't have anything to do with that. And neither does Jonathan. So, if you don't like it—"

"Carter," Jonathan said sternly. "Watch how you speak to your mother."

"I don't want to disrespect her," Carter explained, his tone defensive, "but she's not looking out for my best interests right now. All she wants to do is get back at you for something you had no control over in the first place."

Even at the young age of seventeen, Carter could put two and two together and realize what was really going on. Amanda Washington was a miserable woman who must be a bear to live with. Tamara found herself wondering if the woman had always been like this, or if it had been her husband's infidelity that had made her this way. Then she thought of how loving her mother always was to Tamara and all her siblings—Solomon included. At first, understandably, she hadn't wanted anything to do with Solomon; but it hadn't taken long for her to come around.

Tamara credited her father for continuing to love his wife through the pain she must have felt once she'd discovered that he had another child.

Tamara had been in Amanda Washington's presence for an hour, tops, and the woman had already managed to help her see her dad in a new light. She was suddenly overwhelmed with gratitude that David Davison was the warm, loving man that he was; otherwise, her mother easily could have become just like the bitter, hateful woman seated across from her.

When the server delivered their meals, nobody was more grateful to see a burrito than Tamara. She stuffed her mouth and concentrated on her plate so she wouldn't have to say another word, and she was amazed by her self-restraint when Amanda asked the server for several to-go boxes because she simply couldn't eat all the food she'd ordered.

The check was passed to Jonathan, and he paid it with a smile before the four of them left the restaurant.

Carter nudged his mother as they neared the car. Through clenched teeth, Amanda said, "Thank you for dinner, and thanks for helping Carter."

"You don't have to thank me," Jonathan told her.

"But it's nice to be appreciated," Tamara couldn't resist putting in. "And I'm sure that Jonathan appreciates your acknowledging his generous efforts."

"Wasn't nobody talkin' to you, missy."

For Jonathan's sake, Tamara clamped her mouth shut. But she counted down the fifteen minutes it took to drive Amanda and Carter home, dreading every delay caused by a red light. When they finally reached the house, Jonathan pulled to the curb; at last, the woman got out of the car.

As Carter climbed out after her, Amanda sent one final, parting shot. Pointing across the street at a big pile of rubble, she told Jonathan, "They should have torn that house down a long time ago. If that house hadn't been there, then I wouldn't've had to see your mother's face every morning for twenty years."

While Carter rushed his mother up the walkway and into the house, Jonathan seemed transfixed by the pile of splintered wood and crumbled concrete that had once been his home. It seemed to Tamara that he spent those moments grieving, but she was glad that it had been torn down. No more staring out the window. He could now free himself from the past.

She said as much to him as they started back to the hotel.

"You're right about that," Jonathan said with a nod. "I guess it just caught me off guard to see the house destroyed like that."

"What caught me off guard was the pure meanness of Amanda Washington." Tamara shivered. "I wouldn't want to run across that lady in a dark alley."

"When was the last time you found yourself in any alley, dark or otherwise?" Jonathan asked as he pulled up to a red light.

"You know what I mean. I feel sorry for Carter. I bet he spends a lot of time staring out the window, too."

"I hope not, because that was the loneliest existence imaginable."

Tamara turned to Jonathan. It broke her heart to think of him as a lonely kid with no friends and only his mother to talk to. Not only that, but he'd also had to deal with the fact that he was an illegitimate child. She put her hand on his shoulder. "You know what I wish?"

Smiling at her touch, Jonathan said, "I have no clue. Tell me."

"I wish for your happiness, and no more lonely days for the rest of your life."

"And I wish to take you out again. Because what we just experienced was a lousy excuse for a date."

Tamara settled back in her seat. "Oh, okay. I guess the least you can do is take me out for a nice dinner before we leave this town. And since we are in Louisiana, I don't even want to see a burrito on the menu."

10

Jonathan believed Tamara when she told him that she wasn't interested in a relationship right now. He just didn't understand why a woman as beautiful as she, who had so much to offer, wouldn't want to share her life with someone. He was determined not to pressure her, but, at the same time, this was their last night together in New Orleans, and his plan was to give her the experience of a lifetime—something she would never forget—in hopes that she wouldn't be able to help but keep thinking about him once he was out of sight.

And he knew just the place to take her. When Jonathan was a kid, he and his mother used to walk by the river in Uptown on their way home from collecting cans. By the time they'd finished scrounging around for every can they could find, Jonathan's mouth would be so parched that he'd want to jump in the river and drink the water as if it had come out of the kitchen faucet.

When his stomach would start growling, his mother would remind him about the big pot of stew she'd fixed for them. But he was always so hungry and thirsty that he'd ask her, "Can't we just get something to eat at one of these restaurants?"

His mother's eyes would cloud over with sadness. "I wish I could afford to take you to lunch for all the work you put in today. But Mama's got to pay the electric bill, or you'll be doing your homework by candlelight."

There was always one bill or another that was in urgent need of being paid. Jonathan remembered longing for the day when his mother wouldn't have to worry about bills. The day when she wouldn't have to go out on her day off from work to collect cans to recycle in order to earn a little cash to pay those bills.

The moment he'd start thinking like that, it was as if his mother could read his mind, because she would point at one of the restaurants as they passed and say, "One day, you're gonna own one of these restaurants. And I'll be able to come eat anytime I want to."

"You really think I could have a restaurant of my very own, Mama?" he remembered asking her once.

"I know you can. I'm raising me a real businessman. I can see it in the way you count your money and how you're always finding odd jobs so that you can make a few extra dollars, when most kids your age are out playing in their yards."

His mother's words had given him hope when he'd been too young to know what hope was. But it had been on those walks, collecting cans, that Jonathan had started dreaming about putting his name on one of the nearby buildings. His dreams had expanded as God had enlarged his territory. And Jonathan knew he'd been wise not to open a business in the Uptown area, because he didn't belong in this city anymore.

But that didn't take away the emotional attachment he felt whenever he came to the place where his dreams had been birthed.

Jonathan had finally managed to dine at one of those restaurants before he'd left this town and all the bad memories behind. The summer before he'd moved away to college, he'd been especially diligent about saving his money. There had been only one person on whom he had been willing to spend any of his hard-earned money, and that was his mother. On her birthday, he'd told her to put on her best dress, and he'd taken her to Clancy's. His mother had beamed the entire night. She'd loved the restaurant and her meal, but even more, she had loved telling everyone that her son was a true gentleman.

Tamara wanted to taste New Orleans-style food, and Jonathan was going to make sure she did—at the place where his dreams had begun. It was only fitting, because she had gotten him dreaming again.

⁓

Tamara had shopped all day long, searching for the perfect outfit to wear to dinner with Jonathan. Now butterflies were racing around her stomach as she stood in front of the full-length mirror in her hotel room. She wasn't sure if the dress she'd picked out was appropriate for tonight. Sleeveless and made of white chiffon, it was an attention grabber for sure, with a V-neck and a plunging back.

Taking a deep breath, Tamara tried to settle the flutters in her stomach. She was going out with Jonathan, but there was no reason to be nervous. She stepped away from the mirror, deciding it was too late for second-guessing her choice of attire. This was the only dress she'd purchased today, with shoes and purse to match, and there was no way she was taking it off.

Realizing that she still needed to transfer the contents of her everyday Gucci purse to her new clutch, she sat down on the bed and began emptying the Gucci, taking out her billfold, a tube of lipstick, a hand mirror, and a packet of breath mints. Then she saw it—the letter Belinda had given her.

She had forgotten all about it. In a way, Tamara wanted to shove the letter back inside her purse and forget about it a little while longer—or maybe even forever. She knew that if she read it, she would need to respond in some way, and she wasn't sure she was ready to do that—or if she'd ever be. Belinda's betrayal had occurred a decade ago, but it had hurt, and Tamara wasn't sure that she wanted to relieve any part of that hurt right now.

Tamara glanced at the clock on the nightstand. She had about ten minutes before Jonathan would be knocking on her door. Holding the letter in front of her face, she tossed it around, back and forth. Then, sighing deeply, she decided it was time. She bowed her head and said a quick prayer: "Lord, I thought this wound had already healed, but if I'm having this much trouble with reading a letter from someone who has already apologized to me, then there must still be something there. Help me to forgive and to let it go, God. I want to live just as free as Belinda now seems to be. Thank You, Jesus. Thank You for always hearing me when I pray—even when it's been a while."

Without further delay, Tamara ripped the envelope open, pulled out the paper inside, unfolded it, and started reading the words of someone she had once considered a friend:

Tamara,

I've been trying to build my nerve up to write you this letter for many years now. First, I want to thank you for befriending me back in college. Even though I wasn't a good friend to you, you modeled before my eyes how a true friend treats others.

I have no excuse for the way I acted, so I won't try to come up with one. I never appreciated your friendship as I should have, because I wanted only one thing from you, and that was to get close to Tony so that I could steal his heart away from you. Boy, am I sorry for that. I won't bore you with the details of the miserable life I had with a man I blindly desired far more than I should have. But I will say this: If it had not been for Tony, I probably would still be the same person I was back in college. Yet the humiliation and the agony that were *inflicted on me at the hands of someone who should have loved and cherished me were the very things that sent me in search of a Savior.*

I am happy to say that even though my marriage to Tony was a disaster, and we are now divorced, I have peace in my life because I now know the same Jesus you used to tell me about during our college days. Thank you for letting your light shine back then. When things went so wrong between Tony and me, it was as if God was beginning to remind me of my time spent with you and our talks about the Lord.

I know you're wondering why in the world I would even bother to write to you after what I did, but God has put you on my heart. And I want you to know that I pray for you all the time. I keep praying that God will send someone wonderful into your life, and that, when you finally marry the man of your dreams, you will always feel as if you've found heaven on earth.

Remember that, okay, Tamara? Don't ever settle for anything less. And, if you don't mind, please give me call or write back to let me know when God works that miracle in your life.

Your friend, if you need one,
Belinda

Tears rolled down Tamara's face as she finished reading the letter. Belinda was so different these days, and Tamara was convinced that it was her new life in Jesus Christ that had made the difference. To know that she'd played even a small part in Belinda's transformation gave her newfound appreciation for the foundation of biblical teaching she'd gotten from her father and his skill at making the Scriptures relevant to his congregation. She could still hear him quoting Matthew 5:16: *"Let your light so shine before men, that they may see your good works, and glorify your Father which is in heaven."*

To know that the Word of God her father preached, and Tamara's personal application of that Word, had helped both Belinda and Jonathan was humbling. It was also confusing, for while she still believed everything she'd told Belinda and Jonathan, she had somehow become rather cavalier about her relationship with God.

The knock on her door startled her. Tamara jumped off the bed. "I'm coming," she called as she refolded the letter and shoved it back in her purse. Then she checked her reflection in the mirror, wiping the tears from her face. Her makeup wasn't completely ruined, even if it didn't look quite as flawless as it had a few minutes ago. Hopefully, Jonathan wouldn't notice.

"So, I'm on time, and you're running late?" he said from the other side of the door. "Talk about a role reversal."

Swinging the door open wide, Tamara said, "I don't know what you're talking about. I've been sitting here, waiting on you, for at least ten minutes."

"Wow!" was all Jonathan said as he stood there gazing at her. His eyes traveled upward from her feet to her face, at which point his expression of awe turned to one of concern. "Have you been crying? What's the matter?"

Shaking her head, she told him, "I'm fine, really. Let's just go. I missed lunch, so I'm starving." Brushing past him, she kept walking, hoping that he would take the hint and drop the subject.

He drove her to Uptown, parked at the Uptown/river corner of Annunciation and Webster, and led her into Clancy's, known as being one of the best Creole cuisine restaurants in New Orleans. Tamara was licking her lips as she sat down at the table covered in white linen, just thinking about the gumbo she was about to consume.

By the time their server arrived at their table, they'd both had a chance to look over the menu. Tamara ordered the seared sea scallops and shrimp with a side of gumbo, while Jonathan requested veal stuffed with crabmeat.

"I'm so glad I made reservations," Jonathan said, looking around at the packed space. "It's crowded tonight."

"I guess you bring a lot of women here, huh?"

"Nope. I've come with only one other woman."

Tamara raised an eyebrow at him.

"My mother. I treated her to Clancy's the summer before I left for college."

"Do you miss her?" Tamara asked him. "I can't imagine you see her very often."

"I used to. For a long time, my mother was really the only person I had on my side. But it wouldn't have been fair to her if I required her to move every time I moved my business to a different city. And besides, she wouldn't have met the love of her life if I hadn't moved her down to Florida, where she wanted to live since she was a kid."

"That was nice of you to do that for her." She smiled, then narrowed her eyes. "But I'm not buying this I'm-just-a-lonely-entrepreneur-with-no-one-to-call-my-own act you are trying to sell, either."

Jonathan reared his head back as if he'd just received a serious slap. "Are you calling me a liar?"

"Not necessarily a liar, but maybe one who stretches the truth."

Jonathan laughed from way down deep in his belly. "I love that you say whatever comes to your mind—no filter. But I don't think I'm stretching the truth on this one. And if you don't believe me, I can call my mom and have her verify it."

"Your mom has no idea what you're doing when she's not around. I mean, seriously, Jonathan—a man as handsome and successful as you could have any woman he wanted. And what are you doing? Still playing the field. It must be that you have so many women to choose from, you feel alone, because you haven't yet picked that one special woman to share your life with."

⌇

Tamara had him all wrong. He'd already picked that "one special woman"; she just hadn't picked him.

"I'm too busy to play the field. How could I have built my 'empire,' as you called it—and with 'desperation,' I might add—if I had been running around with all the women your twisted mind is imaging?"

"Maybe 'desperation' was too strong a word," she conceded. "I was just trying to get to the essence of who you are, to figure out the gist of your singular focus."

They bantered back and forth for the rest of the meal, which far exceeded Jonathan's expectations. When they had finished, they both leaned back in their seats and rested their hands over their bellies.

"Now, that was a meal." Tamara beamed. "Thank you for bringing me here. It was so much better than Mexican food."

"Hey, don't knock Mexican food. It's actually a favorite of mine."

"I'm not knocking it. I just don't see a purpose for it in Louisiana."

"Point taken." Jonathan paid the bill, and as they were leaving the restaurant, he said, "I need to walk off some of this food. How about a walk along the Mississippi River?"

Tamara smiled. "Sounds delightful."

Uptown was built along the higher ground around an old natural river levee that followed the wide, gradual bend of the Mississippi. The streets were laid out either roughly paralleling the river's curve or perpendicular to it, resulting in a pattern many described as a "wheel with spokes." As Jonathan strolled the path with Tamara, he was captivated by the sights and smells all around him, but nothing captivated him more than the woman by his side.

As he took her hand in his, a current of emotions coursed through him. He had to close his eyes to get his bearings.

"You okay?" Tamara asked.

His eyes flew open. "I'm good."

"It's lovely out tonight," Tamara said as they continued their walk. "Thank you again for bringing me here. I definitely needed the exercise, and I really enjoy hanging out with you." She smiled up at him. "So many years had passed since our last meeting, I sort of forgot how much fun we used to have together."

"I haven't forgotten anything about those days I spent with you." He swung her hand forward and backward between them.

"Maybe 'forgot' was another instance of a poor word choice. I remember so many details of all the fun we used to have together. And the thing about it was, we used to do a bunch of stuff that didn't cost any money, like taking walks in the park—kind of like we're doing now."

"And don't forget how many times I beat you at Monopoly," Jonathan reminded her.

Tamara shook her head. "That had totally slipped my mind. But I would like to thank you for the countless hours you spent tutoring me in math. If it weren't for you, I probably would have flunked out of my freshman year."

"You're welcome." He put an arm around her shoulders as they stopped and gazed down at the river.

"And thank you for agreeing to the interview. I know that you've kept very private about your business and that you've turned down numerous requests for interviews. So, I appreciate your making me look good at work by saying yes."

"I've never been able to say no to you about anything, Tamara. But you are correct about how private I am about my business. I like to just do what I do without all the fanfare. I don't need to be in the public eye to make construction deals."

"But think how much more business you'll acquire once everyone knows more about you—your upright character, your generous heart. Maybe I should write about this walk you took me on, or those heavily imagined Monopoly wins you boasted about."

He grinned. "Write about whatever makes you happy. I just want to make sure that this isn't over for us." He turned to face her as he added, "You were once very important in my life. I don't want you to leave tomorrow and forget—again—what we once meant to each other."

Shaking her head, Tamara told him, "That could never happen. And now that I know you want to be a part of my life, just try to get rid of me."

Jonathan planted a kiss on her forehead. "That's the last thing I'd ever want to do, Tamara."

"Glad to hear it, because I'm back in your life. For good." She hugged him, then pulled away. "Best friends forever." She held out her pinkie finger so they could do a pinkie swear, like old times.

But Jonathan didn't want to go back to the relationship they'd had in college. He wanted so much more. He'd give it time, but one day, Tamara Davison would be more than just a pinkie-swearing best friend. Much more.

11

Tamara had been back in Atlanta for about three weeks. In that time, she'd completed her piece on Jonathan Hartman and submitted it, earning rave reviews from her boss. She'd also done a final interview with the station's Chicago affiliate and felt fairly confident about how she'd performed, though she had yet to hear one way or the other.

Even with all these positives, she hadn't been able to smile, at least genuinely, since saying good-bye to Jonathan. The truth she was finally able to acknowledge was that she missed Jonathan…and she missed her family. She wanted desperately to visit them, but she had been asked to cover three back-to-back events, leaving her no time for a quick weekend trip home.

"Hey, I hear congratulations are in order," said Maria Sanchez as she strode into the office she shared with Tamara.

"Congratulations? For what?"

"Don't be coy," Maria said, waving her hand in the air. "It's all over the office."

Tamara turned her computer monitor so she could look directly at Maria. "I'm serious when I say that I have no idea what you're talking about."

Maria clamped a hand over her mouth.

Tamara stood to her feet and folded her arms across her chest. "Spill it."

"Oh, I have such loose lips. I'm sure Doug wanted to tell you himself. After all, the decision was partly his. Maybe I shouldn't say anything."

"Out with it, Maria. Doug will be in meetings for the rest of the day, and I'm not waiting till tomorrow to find out something that everybody else apparently knows already."

"Okay, but you didn't hear this from me. Got it?" Maria gave her the evil eye as she waited for a response.

"I didn't hear this from you. Got it."

"You got the job in Chicago!" Maria started jumping up and down, then stopped when she noticed Tamara's failure to jump with her. "What's wrong? I thought you wanted that job!"

"I did. I mean, I do." Tamara walked back to her desk and dropped into her chair, stunned. "I guess I just didn't expect to get it."

"Are you kidding? Our sister company was more than pleased that you were able to score an interview with the elusive Jonathan Hartman."

"Who isn't all that elusive. He's just a regular guy who loves his job and enjoys giving back as an expression of gratitude to God for blessing him so richly."

"What did he tell you about that 'Trouble Man' song? Is it still his fave?"

Tamara had told Maria about her college friendship with Jonathan and had mentioned that she was curious to know if "Trouble Man" was still his favorite song—his theme song, as he'd called it back then. She felt her eyes grow wide. "Oh, no. I forgot to ask him!"

"Calm down, Tamara. It's not the end of the world. It's such a minor detail…one that nobody else would know about. I'm sure the piece is still really good."

Tamara grabbed her purse. "Not good enough. It's not finished." She was a professional, and she couldn't believe she'd forgotten to include that question in the interview. As a journalist, she'd been trained to incorporate the element of surprise into every interview—to ask one question guaranteed to get an answer that just might take the interview someplace new and unexpected. Maybe even to a place worthy of a Pulitzer.

There was a line of lyrics in "Trouble Man" that she needed an answer to. Because if Jonathan still lived by it, then her entire piece was wrong, her conclusions skewed. She had allowed their friendship to influence the way she handled the interview, and that just wasn't who she was. She needed to right this wrong.

"Can you do me a big favor and handle the city council dinner this evening?" she asked Maria. "I need to bring this interview to a close before Doug publishes it."

"I got your back, girl. Go get him."

Tamara rushed to her apartment and threw a few essential items into her overnight bag. She would have to be back in Atlanta by noon tomorrow to ensure she'd have enough time to interview the members of a Christian rock band that was performing in the city tomorrow night. But since Maria had agreed to fill in for her at this evening's event, she should have more than enough time to go home, speak with Jonathan, and even spend a little time with her family before returning to Atlanta in time for her next gig.

As she grasped the doorknob, she turned around and scanned her apartment. This place had never really felt like home—just four walls and a fabulous kitchen with granite countertops. But she'd never hung any pictures on the walls. Never personalized any room. Now she was headed to Chicago, to another place with four walls that was nothing like home. She closed the door and left as a lone tear ran down her face.

It was four-thirty in the afternoon when she reached Charlotte. As she raced up the stairs to Jonathan's office, she prayed that he hadn't left work early. *Not today. Please be here.* Rounding the corner, she came face-to-face with the woman who'd been seated behind the desk outside his office the day she'd tracked Jonathan down three weeks ago. Lisa, if Tamara's memory served her correctly.

"Hi, Lisa, right?" She stuck out her hand to shake the woman's hand. "Is he in?" She asked as if she'd known the woman for years and popped in on Jonathan all the time.

"Yes, Mr. Hartman is in. Can I help you?"

"I was trying to catch him before he left for the day." Tamara kept her voice upbeat, still trying to sound as if she belonged there.

Lisa snapped her fingers. "You're Ms. Davison—the one who did the interview."

"That's me!"

"Do you have an appointment with Mr. Hartman?"

Come on, lady. Don't be a roadblock. "Would you please just tell Jonathan that I'm out here? I'm sure he'll say that it's okay for me to come in and see him."

Lisa picked up her appointment book and checked the day's schedule. "If your name isn't in here, you can't go in there today." She pointed at Jonathan's door. "He is swamped, and he would have my head if I interrupted him for an unplanned meeting."

Tamara didn't want to start an argument at Jonathan's place of business. She should have called ahead or e-mailed, but she'd wanted to surprise him with her presence. Sighing heavily, she turned away from Lisa and was about to head back downstairs to wait for Jonathan to exit the building. Hopefully, it wouldn't be hours before he called it quits for the night.

Just then, she heard a door swing open. "Lisa, I was looking over this draft you just handed me, and something doesn't seem right..." Jonathan's voice trailed off as he stared at Tamara.

She'd come here with the simple goal of getting one question answered, as well as to give Jonathan a little surprise. But as she beheld him for the first time in three long weeks, she was suddenly speechless. His cheeks were shadowed with stubble, making him look ruggedly handsome. His tie hung loosely around his neck, and the top several buttons of his crisp white dress shirt were undone.

"Tamara, what are you doing here?"

"I—I needed to see you," she answered, coming out of her trancelike state.

Jonathan glanced at his watch. "I have a six o'clock meeting, but I can free up a few minutes, if that will work."

She nodded. "That's all I need."

He studied her with a look of puzzlement as he opened his office door wide. "Come on in."

"I'm sorry, Mr. Hartman, but I thought you were too busy to see anyone," Lisa sputtered.

"That's okay, Lisa. I always have time for Tamara."

Lisa looked almost indignant as Tamara brushed past her into Jonathan's office.

He closed the door behind her, and she lowered herself onto the sofa. "She's like a guard dog," she muttered.

"Lisa is very good at her job. She keeps me organized and sane." Jonathan sat down next to her. "Why didn't you call or text to let me know you would be in town this weekend?"

"It was a spur-of-the-moment trip. I wanted to see my family, and also I needed to ask you one more question to finalize our interview."

"So, this is strictly business? Maybe I should put on my jacket and sit behind my desk."

"Don't be like that." Tamara touched his arm and leaned a little closer to him. "I'm happy for the chance to see you again so soon after our last visit. Especially since I just found out that I got the job in Chicago."

"You did? Wow—congratulations, even though it means you're moving even farther away. You came to break the bad news to your family, huh?"

"I wouldn't call it bad news. This gets me to the next level in my career. I'm going to be co-anchoring a weekend style show for a major network. If I can pull this off, my career will skyrocket."

"Well, I'm glad you're happy." Jonathan gave her a smile that looked forced. "I just hope your family will be, too. I know how close you are to them, and I can't imagine they'll be glad to see you move so far away."

Truth be told, Tamara didn't feel much like celebrating, either. She didn't know what was wrong with her. She'd just been given the best news she'd ever received since beginning her career in journalism, and she hadn't smiled about it even once. Maybe she was still in shock over the awesome opportunity she'd earned. Once she moved to Chicago, surely she would be thrilled about her new assignment and the chance to start a whole new life, even if she was far away from her family…and far away from Jonathan.

"Okay, here's the deal. I neglected to ask you about something I remembered about you from college, and I wanted to know if it was still a thing for you now."

Relaxing a bit, Jonathan asked, "What's that?"

"Are you still 'Trouble Man'?"

His eyebrows scrunched as he sat up straight. "Why would I be troubled?"

She gasped. "You don't remember, do you?"

He shook his head. "Remind me."

"When we were in college, you used to borrow my headset to listen to this oldies soundtrack. There was a song on there that you kept rewinding and replaying, and I asked you about it after I listened to the song, and you told me that it spoke to you."

A smile crept across Jonathan's face as he snapped his fingers and bobbed his head. "'Trouble Man' by Marvin Gaye. I had forgotten all about that song."

"I can see why you identified with it back then," Tamara began. "The line that says, 'I come up hard' is the way you felt, right?"

He nodded.

"But there is another line in that song, and I'm wondering if it stuck with you—if it might be the reason you became so successful." Tamara took a deep breath. She knew she might be putting their renewed friendship in jeopardy by asking this question, especially if Jonathan felt that she was attacking him or making wrongful insinuations. But she was a journalist, duty-bound to ask probing questions and to glean honest answers. Committed to giving her readers the full story. So, she pressed on.

"In the song, Marvin Gaye says that he didn't make it by playing by the rules. Since you loved that song so much, I have to ask…what rules did you break on your way to here?"

～

For a long moment, Jonathan just stared at her. Then he stood, walked over to the window, and looked down at the street. He was far above the crowds below, but he still remembered the days when he'd felt so low that he could barely look up to the people who were on eye level with him.

He turned around to face Tamara. "I've never given an interview about my business practices before."

"I know. That's why the network was so happy with me. You made it to *Forbes* magazine without a single interview."

"I refused to do interviews because I didn't want to dredge up the things that I'm not so proud of." Lowering his head, Jonathan massaged his temples. When he met her gaze again, he told her, "Life is complicated, you know. You start out planning to do everything right, but somehow, it's that one thing you miss that can haunt you for the rest of your life."

Looking nervous, Tamara held up a hand. "Forget I asked. I didn't mean to open a can of worms." She stood. "Let me get out of your way so you can prepare for your next meeting."

"Sit down, Tamara." Jonathan came back over to the sofa, took hold of her hand, and sat down beside her. "I want to talk about it—I really do. But I want to talk to Tamara my friend, not Tamara the reporter."

She started to object, but when he pleaded with his eyes, she nodded. "Okay."

"During our interview, you had asked about my first property. I told you about it, but I left out a few details because I was ashamed. The truth is, I ran out of money on that project. The electrical system needed to be replaced, and I knew it, but I couldn't afford it. So, I sold the house anyway. Somehow, it passed inspection. I received my check and paid back the bank, which meant I had enough money to begin my next project, which was located only a block away from the house I'd just sold.

"I think that was God's way of making me own up to what I did, because I had to pass that house every day to go work on the new house—a house that had a lot fewer problems, thankfully."

Tamara kept silent, not interrupting with any questions. He was grateful to have her as a listening ear and nothing else.

Jonathan's eyes began to water, and he blinked away the tears as he continued. "One night, I stayed very late on the job. I was almost finished, and I didn't want to wait another day before completing it."

In spite of his efforts to hold them back, tears now flowed freely down his face. "Before I knew it, I smelled smoke, so I went outside to investigate. The other house was on fire. I didn't see anyone run outside, so I starting to panic, thinking that the family who'd bought that dump of a place from me was all dead, and it was my fault. I ran down to the house, kicked in the front door, and found the man who'd purchased the house stretched out on his bed, unconscious. I pulled him outside to the front lawn. One of the neighbors came over and called nine-one-one on his cell phone."

Tamara's expression was a mixture of shock and horror. "Was anyone else in the house?"

Jonathan shook his head. "Fortunately, the homeowner's wife had taken the kids to visit her mom that weekend."

"Thank God for that."

"Yes, God was good to all of us that night."

Tamara raised her eyebrows. "What do you mean?"

"I went to the hospital and waited while the doctors worked on Hank. I thought for sure that the police would come to the hospital and arrest me once they determined that the fire had been caused by faulty wiring. But once the smoke had cleared, the fire marshal discovered that Hank had left a pot of food cooking on the stove. The wires in the wall did burn up, but no one ever connected it to me. I went home relieved, thinking that I had caught a lucky break. But I couldn't sleep—not that night, nor any of the nights to come—because I knew in my heart that if Hank hadn't left that food on the stove, the house eventually would have gone up in flames, anyway."

"But you were in the clear," Tamara pointed out. "You should have been thankful that the house burned down for the reason it did. At least no one got hurt."

"True, but my conscience wasn't clear. I lived in torment for about a year, plagued by guilt. I kept buying homes, flipping them, and selling them, but I couldn't sleep. Finally, one day, I said 'Forget it' and went back to that house to check on the family."

Tamara frowned. "I thought you said the house burned up."

"It did, but I was hoping that their insurance would have covered the repairs and that they would be living there again. I guess I really wanted to know if all the wires had been replaced.

"But nothing had been done to the house. It was just this eyesore that sat in the midst of a neighborhood in desperate need of revitalization. I knocked on the neighbor's door and asked him what had become of Hank. And the story he told…it broke my heart." His eyes filled with tears once more.

Tamara gasped and brought her hand to her heart. "He didn't die, did he?"

"Not physically, but his spirit had. His wife and children had never returned. They stayed about an hour away with the wife's mother, and Hank was now homeless, finding refuge in shelters or in his car."

"And you blamed yourself for what happened to him?"

"Not entirely, because I soon discovered that Hank was an alcoholic. He'd been drunk the night he'd left his food to burn on the stove. The insurance company didn't pay him any money because of his actions, not mine. But meeting Hank changed my life."

"How so?" Tamara asked. "Don't worry—I won't write about it, although I wish you'd let me. But I would have thought that you would have been the one to change his life—not the other way around."

Jonathan smiled wistfully. "Let's just say that we helped each other. He is now the head foreman on most of my construction projects…but that's another story. The one you want to hear about is how I found Hank one night as he was checking himself into a homeless shelter. Even though his neighbor had told me about his drinking problem, I didn't smell an ounce of liquor on him, nor did he look like he'd been drinking. He simply looked down on his luck, like life was beating on him, but he was fighting back, and fighting back hard."

"I wonder what had happened to make him clean up his act," Tamara mused.

"I wondered, too. So, after reminding him who I was, I asked him. And do you know what he said?"

She watched him expectantly.

"Hank just smiled as he told me, 'I finally stopped fighting the inevitable.' I didn't understand what he was talking about, so I asked him to clarify. That's when he told me that his wife had been praying for him for years. Hank said that when he finally hit rock bottom, he got on his knees and asked Jesus to come into his heart. Hank didn't need a program to get him to kick his habit. He told me he threw away half a bottle of Jim Beam that night and hadn't touched alcohol ever since."

"Then you felt better, right? Because you knew he'd be okay?" Tamara asked.

He shook his head. "I still felt like crud, because I hadn't mustered the courage to tell Hank the truth about his house. And I kept feeling like I was supposed to do something to help him and his family. That's when I decided to rebuild his house. I met up with Hank again and asked if he had time to help me with the project. He was thrilled, because he was working only part-time and didn't have the money to get the supplies needed to repair the home himself.

"That's how I discovered how handy Hank is. We finished his house, and his family moved back home again. Hank worked with me on my next three projects before I finally got the guts to tell him that I'd known about the faulty wiring in the house when I sold to him."

"How did he react?" Tamara asked, eyebrows raised.

"He reacted in a way that attested to the genuine nature of his God-initiated transformation: by completely forgiving me. And then, he even prayed for me. He told me that God had called me to be a better man than that, and when he said those words, it was as if a fire had been ignited. I broke down, because I had promised God long before that if He would make a way for me, I would make a way for others. But then, the first chance I'd gotten, I'd cut corners that could have cost a good man and his family their very lives.

"I gave my life to the Lord that day. And I was finally able to get a good night's sleep, because I was no longer riddled with guilt."

Tamara studied him with a look he'd never seen before. "I wish you had told me all this before I turned in my interview. It's such an awesome story, and even if I didn't include all the details, I would have taken a totally different approach to the piece."

"I guess I can't stop you from writing about it now," Jonathan murmured. "Not since I was fool enough to lay it all out for you."

She reached for him, but he pulled back.

"You misunderstood me," she told him. "I'm not going to write about this and betray your trust. Even if these details would make the article ten times better than it is right now."

Feeling a strong sense of conviction, Jonathan stood and looked at Tamara with intensity, "You go on and write the whole story. I'm tired of hiding from my past. It's time I let the world know that I'm not as unimpeachable as it would seem." He walked over to his door and opened it. "See you later. I need to prepare for my next meeting."

12

Later that evening, at her parents' house, Tamara could hardly concentrate; her mind was heavily burdened with thoughts of whether she should concern herself with advancing her career or with being a true friend.

Jonathan had given her the okay to write everything he'd told her, but Tamara could tell that he didn't want to see his past laid out in print for the world to read. Even though it was evident to him and to her how God had worked in the situation to bring about ultimate good, today's generation didn't understand divine movements in the lives of believers when anything untoward occurred along the way. The majority of readers would see only the dishonest manner in which Jonathan had handled his first business deal and assume that he was still cutting corners to get ahead.

Tamara didn't believe that one bit, and she didn't want anyone else reaching that conclusion, either. She believed in the power of redemption, or at least she used to...before she'd learned that her own father had broken some rules of his own.

Life could be so complicated. Why couldn't she just tell herself that Jonathan's past was off limits? That no one needed to know what had happened so long ago? Was her career that much more important than loyalty that she would betray a friend to buoy her reputation as a reporter? Her boss had been fine with the original article she'd submitted, so there was really no need to go back and add anything to the story...right?"

"Girl, your mind must be going a mile a minute." Her mother pointed at the paper napkin in Tamara's hands. "You've pretty much ripped that thing to shreds."

"Oh, I'm just thinking about some things." She tossed the napkin in the trashcan. "I came here tonight because there's something I need to tell you and Daddy."

Bishop Davison had been reclining in his chair and watching the nightly news. He turned off the television and swiveled his chair around. "Is something wrong, baby girl? I wondered why you drove home out of the blue like this."

"For one thing, I had been missing all of you." Tamara quieted for a moment, chewing her lip as she tried to figure out how to say what she wanted to say. Finally, she decided that the best thing to do would be to just spit it out. "And I came to tell you that I received a promotion."

"Oh my goodness! That's wonderful." Her mother jumped out of her seat and wrapped her in a hug.

But her father remained in his chair, his eyes trained on Tamara. "Is there more to this promotion?"

"What do you mean, Daddy?"

"Something in your eyes...I don't know what it is, but I get the feeling that you're not sure whether you should accept this offer."

Her father had always been able to read her like a book. She should have known that he would pick up on her hesitation. If she wasn't ready to spill her guts, then she shouldn't have come. Sighing deeply, she told them, "The position is in Chicago."

"Oh, Lord Jesus." Her mother threw her hands in the air. "How much more does that job of yours want from this family? First, they move you to Atlanta, and now they want you all the way in Chicago?"

"Alma, honey." Now her father stood and put a hand on his wife's shoulder. "I don't think it was the job that moved Tamara to Atlanta." He turned to Tamara. "Was it, baby girl?"

He was looking at her like he'd opened her mail and read all her personal business. She loved her father because he had always been so good to her. But it was the fact that he hadn't always been good to her mother that needled Tamara. "What do you want me to say, Daddy?"

"I want you to talk to us. Your mother and I have been praying, but we need you to tell us what's troubling you."

Since her earliest years, the man now standing there, asking her to speak her mind, had been her rock. She'd adored her father for as long as she could remember. And so, even though the discovery of his flaws had hurt her deeply, Tamara hadn't known how to tell a man like her father that she was disappointed in him. She'd left town to avoid having to confront him.

"Baby, what's wrong?" her mother asked, her tone frantic. She pulled Tamara onto the couch with her and started rubbing her back.

Tamara tried to hold back the tears, but they came cascading down her face, anyway. She hadn't meant for their evening to go like this. All she'd wanted was to see her parents, tell them that she was moving to Chicago, then return to Atlanta to pack. But now her father was praying, and her mother was looking her in face, asking for the truth.

"I...I don't want to disrespect you or Daddy, so I'd rather not talk about this tonight. Is that okay?"

Apparently her father wasn't going to let her off that easily. "Tamara, we give you the freedom to speak your mind. You won't be disrespecting us, but you will help to ease some of our worries if you tell us what's bothering you."

She sniffed and took a deep breath. "Daddy, you know I love you, right?" She was crying so hard, her lower lip quivered.

"I know you do. But I also know that things have changed between you and me. Never in a million years would I have guessed that, of our children, you would be the one who would move away and barely come see about your parents, or even call, for that matter."

Her mother was nodding in agreement. "I know your career is important to you, Tamara, but you've got only one mama and one daddy. When we're gone, that's it," her mother said.

Now she felt even worse about the decisions she'd made over the last few years. Not so long ago, her father had suffered a heart attack that had nearly taken him home to glory. What if something happened to him while she was almost twelve hours away from home?

"It's not just about my career, Mama," she began, then took a deep breath. "I'm sorry, but I'm still mad at Daddy for cheating on you. And I'm mad at you because you're the reason the existence of my half brother was kept secret for so long.

"I don't have the kind of relationship with Solomon that I had with Adam, and I doubt I ever will. I think that things could have been so different if the two of you had just been honest from the start."

"Oh, baby." Her mother wrapped her arms around her, trying to soothe her. "You never said a thing—I had no idea you were angry with us." She sat back and wiped some of the tears from Tamara's face. Then she kissed her cheek. "I'm sorry. I never meant to hurt any of you. And your father certainly didn't mean to hurt me when he got involved with Solomon's mother. We both were young and dumb back then."

"Can I interject something, Alma?" Tamara's father asked as he seated himself on her other side.

"Of course, dear. Say whatever is on your mind."

He nodded, then turned to Tamara. "While your mom is correct about the 'young and dumb' part, I want to tell you truthfully that my getting involved with Sheila was partly in order to hurt your mother. I was angry that she and I just couldn't get along; she wanted nothing to do with me. I truly thought she was going to divorce me. I had no idea that we would get back together after she asked for a separation. So, I went out to a club one night with an attitude that said, 'I'll show *her*.' But nothing good comes from things like that, and your mom and I have paid the price for my folly. Even so, we never stopped to consider just how much Solomon and the rest of you kids would eventually pay."

"I know you and Mama weren't very far along in your faith when all your drama occurred," Tamara conceded, "but it still hurts me to know that you are now a man of God, even after doing your dirt."

Her father cleared his throat. "Have you ever heard of a little concept called forgiveness?"

She felt a stab of conviction. She'd readily accepted the concept of forgiveness when Jonathan had told her, just a few hours ago, that God had forgiven him for the criminally negligent way he'd handled his first property. God had even used Jonathan's guilt, repentance, and subsequent forgiveness to put him in a position to bless the lives of others. So, why shouldn't the same be possible for her father? Why should he be disqualified from blessing the lives of the people God had sent him to minister to, just because of a sin he'd committed—and repented of— decades ago?

Suddenly, she felt the weight of her hypocrisy in allowing for forgiveness for others but wishing it'd been withheld from her own mother and father. "I'm sorry, Daddy. You are so right. And, as you always say, '*If the Son therefore shall make you free, ye shall be free indeed.*' Who am I to hold this thing over your head, especially when God has long since forgiven you for it? I hope you can forgive *me* for being such a brat."

"We will forgive each other," her mother said as she hugged Tamara again.

Her father put his arms around both of them. "Forgiven and free, indeed."

After his last meeting for the day, Jonathan went home, cooked a frozen meal in the microwave, and ate it in the privacy of his bedroom. Dredging up the details of his past—how he'd come to discover that he was a sinner in need of divine grace, just like everyone else on God's green earth—had drained him.

All through his meeting with the city officials whose approval he would need for the next project on his list, Jonathan kept thinking that he had ruined everything. No city official in his or her right mind would ever let him construct another building in the local vicinity—or anywhere else across the nation—once Tamara's article came out.

Why had he been so dumb as to make himself vulnerable before a reporter, especially one who was so career-minded, she'd probably throw him under the bus without a thought of how that information might affect his future business deals? *Because you're in love, you big dope,* he said to himself in answer.

He set his empty food tray on the floor, lay down in bed, and pulled the blankets over his body as he thought about the torch he'd carried for Tamara Davison ever since their first week of college. And now, even though they were both single, Tamara was still unavailable. Maybe it was time for him to move on, to find someone who could love him for who he was, flaws and all. What he wanted to do was to fall into a deep sleep and let God cast his sins into the sea of forgetfulness once again.

As his head hit the pillow, Jonathan closed his eyes and prayed that sleep would overtake him quickly. Instead, he tossed and turned as he wondered when everything he'd worked so hard to build would come crumbling down.

An hour later, having had no success with sleep, Jonathan climbed out of bed, got down on his knees, and called out to God. "Lord Jesus, I really need You right now. Please comfort me, because I have nowhere else to turn. You have always been my place of refuge, and I thank You for that. In Jesus' name, amen."

Getting back in bed, Jonathan closed his eyes. Sleep didn't come quickly, but when it did, he was at peace until he opened his eyes early the next morning. His mind tried to drift back to the problems he'd created for himself by being a lovesick pup, but Jonathan refused to go there. He hopped out of bed, threw on a black and white Nike jogging suit, and went for a run.

The wind in his face felt soothing, especially with the reduced humidity, characteristic of the end of September. The autumn months brought perfect running weather to Charlotte. Granted, the winter months weren't so bad, since the temperature rarely fell too far below thirty degrees on even the coldest days. The summer was the worst time for running; the humidity was almost unbearable, and while a few die-hards would faithfully hit the trails in the worst of the heat, Jonathan stayed away during that time.

He waved to each runner he passed, many of them familiar from previous mornings on the path. Smiling at the rewards of exertion, he continued to push himself to do one more lap—and then another. All the while, he thought about the many things he loved about this city: sporting events, especially those involving the Panther's and the Hornet's games; Christian concerts; and the reputation and success his company enjoyed. Hartman Industries had established a well-respected brand among the local populace, and he didn't want to jeopardize that.

At the end of his final lap, Jonathan stopped to retie his shoelaces before the walk home. Maybe he should call Tamara and ask her not to print the information he'd divulged. But he didn't want to beg her for any favors. If their friendship meant so little to her that she would willingly destroy a reputation he'd spent years building, then he would step back and let her do it.

"Jonathan?"

He stood and found himself face-to-face with Savannah Morgan, an attractive young marketing executive he'd met when he'd first arrived in the city. They'd gone out twice, but Jonathan hadn't called her for a third date.

He smiled. "Good morning, Savannah. I haven't seen you all summer. How've you been?"

"Fine, thanks. I haven't been out running, but since the weather is cooling off, I figured I'd get back into it."

"Same here," he said, still grinning.

"You want to run together?"

"I just finished," Jonathan said honestly. "I wish I had known that you were coming out here this morning, because it would have been great to run with you."

"Is that a fact?" Savannah asked, her tone flirtatious.

Pulling his car keys out of his pocket, Jonathan nodded. "Them be the facts."

Savannah started jogging in place, apparently ready to resume her run. "Are you busy next weekend?"

Jonathan couldn't think of a thing he had to do or a person he needed to see that might prevent him from being able to spend time with Savannah. "My schedule is open. What did you have in mind?"

"I have two tickets to the Panthers game. I was getting ready to sell them on StubHub, because I didn't want to go by myself; but if you're interested, I'd love for you to join me."

"Tell you what," Jonathan said. "I'll buy the tickets from you, and then I'll pick you up and take you to dinner before the game. How does that sound?"

"You don't have to buy the tickets."

"I want to. If we're going on a date, I plan to pay. So, what will it be?"

"What if I wanted to treat you to the game?"

He shook his head. "You're too pretty to have to treat an old scrub like me to anything. Let me buy the tickets, and you can treat yourself to something at the mall with the money."

"Okay, okay. You can purchase the tickets from me." She beamed at him. "Give me a call this week so we can make the arrangements." Then she waved and jogged off.

Jonathan stood there watching her as she moved down the trail. Savannah wasn't as beautiful as Tamara, but, in all fairness, he doubted he'd ever find any woman whose beauty matched Tamara's.

But he was thinking with his head instead of his heart now, and his head was telling him it was time to move on. As far as Jonathan was concerned, Savannah Morgan was another prayer answered.

13

Opening the door of her Chicago apartment, Tamara greeted Leah and Larissa with huge hugs. "What's up, divas?"

"Hey, divas in the house!" Larissa sang as she danced her way inside.

Tamara laughed. "I don't know how to thank you two for coming all the way out here to help me unpack all my junk."

"Well, you'd better find a way, because it's only October, and it's already too cold in this city," Leah told her. "I don't do Midwest winters, so don't expect me to be back until springtime."

"How about pizza and a movie?" Tamara suggested. "Will that be an adequate expression of gratitude?"

"Make it deep dish, and you won't hear another complaint from me," Leah said.

Larissa rubbed her stomach. "The baby likes the sound of that. Extra pepperoni, please?"

Laughing, Tamara closed the door behind them. "Just get in here and get to work."

The three of them spent the afternoon emptying the dozens of boxes of Tamara's clothes, household goods, and decorative knickknacks. Each time they came across a family picture and asked where to hang it, Tamara told them to leave it in the box. Finally, Larissa said, "What gives? Are you ashamed of us or something?"

Tamara set down the box that she had just carried into the kitchen. "No, I'm not ashamed of my family. I never hung those pictures when I lived in Atlanta, either. I need for the place to feel like home before I can do something like that. Otherwise, I'd burst into tears every time I walked past them."

"Sounds like somebody is homesick," Leah said. "Is that what I'm hearing from Ms. Chi-Town superstar?"

Tamara rolled her eyes. "I am hardly a superstar. I'm just cohosting some frilly old weekend program. And we all know that most people spend their weekends shopping, not watching TV. I can't imagine there are many people who tune in." She sat down on a kitchen stool and propped her elbows on the counter, resting her chin on her hands. "I don't even know what I'm doing here."

"Hey, don't be so down on yourself." Larissa walked over to Tamara and put an arm around her shoulders. "I have some fantastic news that I was going to wait until later to share with you, but if it will make you feel better, I'll go on and tell you now."

"I already know that you're pregnant, and that you're married to a wonderful man who adores you. What more do you need to rub in my face?"

"Hold on," Leah said, joining them in the kitchen. "Tamara, I thought you said you didn't want a husband or kids or anything of those things."

"I don't," Tamara said quickly. "I'm just saying, single working girls don't want to hear about happily married people all the time."

"Well, you're in luck, because my fantastic news has to do with Carter Washington."

"Carter?" Tamara hit her forehead with the palm of her hand. "I forgot to ask Jonathan about his half brother the last time I spoke with him. That probably gave him one more reason to think I'm just an insensitive jerk."

"Did you and Jonathan get into a fight or something?" Leah asked.

"Not really a fight, just a disagreement. But I don't want to talk about that."

"Then let me tell you the good news," Larissa said. "Solomon was able to get the charges dropped against Carter."

"You're kidding! Your husband is truly the man." She wanted to call Jonathan and celebrate the good news with him over the phone, but she wasn't sure if he wanted to hear from her. He certainly hadn't made contact when she'd had the magazine send him a draft of their interview for his final approval. That act alone had told her everything she needed to know about where they stood.

"And to think that mean old woman doubted him."

"What mean old woman?" Larissa demanded, her hands on her hips.

"Carter's mother, Amanda Washington. Believe me when I tell you, you don't want none of her. I tried to set her straight, but her mouth was more than I could handle. How did Solomon manage it, anyway?"

"They found the gun used to shoot Philip Washington, and the prints on it weren't Carters; they belonged to some gangbanger who had been friends with one of Carter's older brothers. He was arrested, and Carter was cleared of all charges."

"I'm so glad. Carter really is a good kid. Now he can go to college and get away from that hateful mother of his." Tamara shivered at the thought of the woman and the disrespectful way she'd treated Jonathan. Then she wondered what Jonathan thought of the way she, Tamara, had treated him. Did he suspect her of posing as a friend in order to secure an interview and advance her career?

The next day, she received all the mail that had been forwarded from her place in Atlanta. Jonathan had sent her a card, thanking her for recommending Solomon's legal services for his little brother. She smiled at the gesture, then picked up the phone to call him.

When the call went to his voicemail, she almost hung up without leaving a message, but the beep came so quickly, she was caught off guard and started speaking. "H-hey, Jonathan. It's Tamara. I got your card today, and I'm so happy that everything worked out for Carter. Please give him a big hug for me, and tell him that I'm rooting for him. I know he's going to make a big success of his life. Well, I guess that's all I wanted to say... Give me a call back if you want to talk."

After ending the call, she remembered that she'd meant to ask if he'd read the draft the office had sent to him. If he had, he must not have cared for it, or he would have mentioned it in the card, if not sent her a separate card altogether.

Sighing, Tamara started shuffling around her apartment in search of something to do. Leah and Larissa had gone to the mall, but she hadn't had any energy for shopping after a night of unpacking boxes. She decided to get back to business organizing her things. When she uncovered a box of pictures, she noticed a photo album that she hadn't seen in years. It was filled mostly with pictures from her college years.

Sitting down beside the box, she lifted out the album and held it in her lap. As she opened it and flipped through page after page, she noticed one recurring theme...Jonathan. At least for her freshman and sophomore years, he had been there with her through most of the ups and the downs. One particular picture stood out among the rest. In the photo, Tamara's eyes were red. She remembered why: She had just spent the night crying over yet another failed relationship with a cheating jock. Big surprise.

Jonathan had hung out with her all the next day. He'd comforted her and made her forget about her bleeding heart. Before she knew what was happening, Tamara had leaned over and kissed him. He'd pulled her closer, and their lips had stayed together for a long moment. Seizing the photo opportunity, her roommate had run and grabbed her camera. She'd snapped the picture just after their lips had parted and they had moved away from each other.

Nothing had been said about the kiss; Jonathan had simply put an arm around her, and they'd sat snuggled up on the couch watching reruns of *I Love Lucy*. Her mother had loved that show, and Tamara had gotten hooked as a kid. It wasn't a show that Jonathan cared for, but he sat there anyway, watching episode after episode.

She'd thought that it was because of their friendship that he'd stayed and watched the show with her. But now, as she studied the picture, she noticed something she hadn't picked up on before. While her eyes had been red from crying, Jonathan's eyes had been full of obvious love and adoration. A couple of months back, Jonathan had admitted that he'd been in love with her when they were in college. Now, Tamara wondered how different her life might have been if she had noticed back then what was plain to see in this photo. Shaking her head, she closed the photo album and put it back in the box, wishing Jonathan were here with her, rather than some old memories.

⁓

"Aren't you going to call her back?" Carter asked after Jonathan had played Tamara's voicemail message on speakerphone.

Once the police had arrested the right person, Carter had been free to go where he wanted, so he'd called Jonathan and asked if he could come and live with him until it was time to head off to college. He would be starting in the spring semester, so it would be for only a couple of months. Jonathan had jumped at the chance to spend more time with his little brother. Now, the condo didn't feel so lonely with someone else milling around.

"I can't call her right now," Jonathan replied. "I've got to get ready for my date."

"I thought we were going to hang out tonight."

"Didn't I tell you? I have tickets to the Tye Tribbett concert."

Carter's eyes bugged out. "I wouldn't have minded going to that concert. I wish you had said something."

"Sorry, little bro, but I purchased the tickets before you came to town. I'll be on the lookout for something else we can do together, okay?"

"That sounds like a plan. Just tell me that you aren't going out with Savannah again."

"Yes, Savannah 'again.' She's good people. I don't understand what you have against her," Jonathan said as he headed to his bedroom to freshen up.

"She's not Tamara, that's what I have against her. You belong with Tamara. I don't know why you refuse to listen to me."

Every time Carter asked him about Tamara, it was like getting poked with a red-hot needle. He had to put a stop to it, or he wouldn't be able to let Carter stay with him another day. Jonathan spun around and practically barked out his response: "She doesn't want me. I've been in love with that woman since college, and she has never reciprocated my feelings. So let it go, okay? I have to move on, for my own peace of mind."

"Sorry, Bro," Carter said, hands in the air. "I had no idea. I won't mention her again."

"Thank you."

Jonathan took a shower and tried to stop Tamara from taking up space in his head. He let the hot, steamy water beat down on his head, trying to drown himself in a pool of forgetfulness. But no matter how much he tried to escape thoughts of Tamara, his mind continued to betray him. Soon he was reliving a weekend from junior year as if it had happened yesterday...

Everybody on campus was amped up because of homecoming. Jonathan was seated in the stands, watching the football game, but his attention was mostly on Tamara, standing on the sidelines with the other members of the cheerleading squad.

Mr. All-American had broken her heart earlier that week, when Tamara had discovered that he'd been cheating on her with another cheerleader.

With pom-poms raised, Tamara and the rest of the squad chanted, "Watch out, boy, because we're here…we're here to cheer…."

As the chant continued, Tamara was smiling outwardly, doing a good job of pumping up the crowd, but he could tell that she wasn't okay. And it was in that moment that he decided he'd sat idly by long enough. He didn't want her to get played by another baller at this school. And after the way she had kissed him just a few days prior, he figured it was time that he let her know how he truly felt about her. Their friendship had to mean something to Tamara. As close as they had become over the past two years, he believed in his heart that she cared just as deeply about him as he did about her. He just had to convince her that she could have a wonderful life with a regular Joe like him, rather than trying to find her self-worth in being some baller's girl.

The game was almost over, and their team was winning, the crowd pulsating with excitement. Jonathan started making his way down the bleachers. The quarterback took off, shuffling his feet, faking to the left, then went straight down the field.

Everybody jumped up to cheer him on. "Go, go, go," they all chanted. Then it happened: Touchdown! And it was over. They had won, and everybody was jumping up and down.

Jonathan was excited, too, but more about getting to Tamara. He had to tell her how he felt. They were meant to be together. She was his forever love.

But as he reached the field, Mike Barnes, the tight end on the team, pulled Tamara into his arms and kissed her.

"What was that for?" Tamara asked when he finally ended the kiss.

"I've been wanting to do that since last year," he confessed. "Now that you finally dropped that zero, I was hoping you were in need of a hero."

Don't fall for it, Tamara! Jonathan wanted to scream the words, but instead he stood there watching, hoping, and praying that she would back away from Mike and turn to him.

Tamara smiled and kissed Mike again. "My hero," she practically purred, as he held her in his arms.

Shoulders slumping, Jonathan trudged off the field and across campus to his dorm. When he reached his room, he lay on his bed and closed his eyes, trying to block out the pain of feeling as if he'd been stuck looking out another

*window, wondering what life was like on the other side. That night, he made
a decision: He would never be that lurker again. He was going to go out and
make a life for himself and let the rest of the world look at and wonder about
him.*

Turning off the water, Jonathan slammed his fist against the wall.
"Forget this." He stepped out of the shower. "I'm not going to stand
around here in misery." He dressed and headed out for a night on the
town with a woman who actually saw him and wanted to be with him.
That was good enough.

⌒

Carter might have promised not to mention Tamara to his brother
anymore, but he hadn't promised not to talk to her himself. From the
first time he'd seen Tamara and Jonathan together, when he'd watched
her defend Jonathan from his mother's verbal attacks, he'd known that
the two of them had something special. Why his brother was refusing
to see the truth, Carter didn't know. But he was about to find out.

Having gotten Tamara's number from Jonathan's cell phone while
he'd been in the shower, he punched the digits into his own phone and
placed the call.

Tamara picked up on the third ring. Smiling to himself, Carter said,
"Thanks for asking Jonathan about me, Ms. Davison."

She hesitated a moment, then said, "Carter? Is that you?"

"It's me. Jonathan and I listened to your message a little while ago."
Yes, he was throwing his brother under the bus, and he knew it. But it
was for Jonathan's own good. "I really appreciated what you said about
me."

"I meant every word of it. You were temporarily derailed, but never
forget that your father wanted you to make something of yourself; and
with Jonathan as a big brother, I'm confident that you'll be able to do
anything you put your mind to."

"Yeah, my big bro is really something." He let those words hang
there a moment and waited for her to respond.

"Where is that big brother of yours? I was hoping that he would call me back so I could talk to him."

That was what he'd wanted to hear. "I'm sure he'll call when he has a chance," he replied. "Right now, he's at a concert with Savannah. That woman barely lets him have any time to himself anymore."

"Savannah?" He could hear the frown in her tone. "I don't remember Jonathan mentioning anyone by that name."

"He probably didn't. I wonder why. The two of them have been together for a while. Looks like it's about to get serious."

"Oh," was all Tamara said. The line went silent.

"Hello, Ms. Davison? Are you still there?"

Carter grinned to himself, for now he knew for sure that he was right about Jonathan and Tamara. But how was he going to get the two of them to see what was right in front of them?

"I'm here," she finally replied, "but I think I'd better hang up now. I'm busy getting my apartment in order, and then I'm going to hit the town with my sisters and see how much damage we can do to Chicago."

"Okay, well, don't forget to call Jonathan back," Carter told her. "I'm sure he'd love to hear from you."

"Do me a favor, Carter. Don't mention that you and I talked. And please don't tell Jonathan that I want him to call me back."

"But I thought you said—"

"I know what I said, Carter. But just forget it. Okay?"

He wasn't allowed to bring her up to Jonathan, anyway. "Okay, I won't say anything. But you really need to call him."

"Have fun at school, Carter. Go out and set the world on fire," she said before ending the call.

14

Tamara didn't understand why she was crying, but sadness had somehow crept up on her during her conversation with Carter. She'd rushed to get off the phone because she hadn't wanted to start sobbing while still talking to him. The last thing she needed was for Carter to tell Jonathan that she'd blubbered over the phone when she'd learned that he was out on a date. She shouldn't be crying, anyway; she ought to be happy that Jonathan had finally found someone to share his life with. Wasn't that what she'd always wanted for him?

But Jonathan was a scoundrel and a liar. She wasn't about to be happy for him and some other woman. After giving a good kick to the box containing the album of photos from college, she picked up her cell phone and was about to hurl it across the room when she heard the doorbell ring. Her heart was still brimming with anger as she stormed over to the door and opened it. Before Leah and Larissa had taken even a step inside, she blasted them with a furious question: "Why did he kiss me if he already had a girlfriend?"

"Whoa, wait a minute," Leah said as she set her bags on the floor. "Who are you talking about?"

"Why don't you sit down, Tamara?" Larissa suggested as she tiptoed inside. "You look like you're about to blow." She took Tamara by the arm and led her down the hall toward the sofa.

"Men are such cheaters...dogs," Tamara declared.

"What happened? Will you please tell us what's going on?" Leah bent down in front of her sister, tissue in hand, and wiped the tears from Tamara's face. "And stop crying, okay? I don't like to see you hurting. It makes me want to cry, too."

Taking the tissue from her sister, Tamara blotted her eyes. "I thought he was different...a real prince of a guy. Especially after he fed me that whole 'born again' line. But Jonathan is just like everyone else."

Larissa and Leah exchanged glances. They sat down on either side of Tamara. Then Larissa said, "I thought you and Jonathan were just friends."

"We are just friends." Getting frustrated, Tamara said, "At least, I thought we were friends."

"Then why are you so upset over the fact that he apparently has a girlfriend?" Leah asked.

"He..." Taking a deep breath, she began again. "The whole time I was in New Orleans with him, Jonathan never said one word about a girlfriend. Not when he asked me out to dinner, not when we strolled by the river holding hands, and certainly not when he kissed me."

Rubbing her back, Larissa said, "I'm sorry that happened to you. I really thought Jonathan was a nice guy. I'm surprised by his behavior."

"That's just it—none of them is a true-blue nice guy. Not Daddy, not Adam, and probably not even Solomon. They all cheat."

Larissa held up her hand. "Now wait just a minute. I'm not going to let you call Uncle David a cheater. I believe he was saved by God's grace and that he has not cheated on Aunt Alma since that one time over thirty years ago.

"And as for my husband, I will not let you put something on him that does not belong there simply because you're upset with Jonathan. Solomon is a good, faithful man, and I'm blessed to have him. End of story."

"You know you've stepped out of bounds when you get Larissa all riled up—she rarely gets angry about anything," Leah scolded Tamara. "You need to apologize."

Nodding, Tamara turned to her sister-in-law. "Leah's right. I was out of line. I know that Daddy isn't a cheater and that Solomon loves you way too much to ever do something like that. I'm just mad at the world and taking it out on my family once again."

"Well, you might be right about Adam," Leah interjected. "From what I'm hearing, Portia has contacted a divorce attorney because she thinks Adam is spending way too much time at Carla and Britney's house."

Tamara shook her head. "Maybe he's trying to help Carla get her life back on track so she can be a positive influence for her daughter." She really didn't like Portia and wished that Adam hadn't married the woman in the first place.

"Or maybe he just doesn't like being in the same house with the woman who almost got him killed," Larissa mused. "Can you imagine? The poor thing must sleep with one eye open."

"Adam probably hasn't had a full night's sleep in the past two years," Leah agreed. "It's crazy. I have no idea why he stays in the same house with that nutcase."

"I guess it's easy for us to criticize," Larissa reasoned, "but Adam is just trying to keep the vows he spoke before God. And, as Kerry Washington said in *Save the Last Dance*, 'Ain't no shame or blame in that.'"

"Preach it, Larissa." Tamara laughed. "Or should I call you Kerry Washington? Got any scandals we should know about?"

"The only scandal I'm dealing with is what's going on right here." She playfully nudged Tamara's shoulder. "Why in the world did you pretend you weren't interested in Jonathan, when you are obviously crazy about him?"

Tamara sighed. "I wasn't pretending. I just didn't know how I felt about him until recently. But it doesn't matter, because he's not really into me like that anymore."

"How would you know?" Leah demanded.

Tamara tapped her temple with her fingertip, as if she were thinking hard. "Let's see…could it be because he has a girlfriend?" There was that other part about Jonathan's thinking she cared more about advancing her career than about him, but she didn't want to get into that with her family.

Larissa groaned. "You're being silly, Tamara. No man is taken until he's wearing a wedding ring. Are they engaged?"

"I don't know," she answered honestly. "But Carter made it sound like they were serious."

"Carter just moved in with Jonathan. He might not be aware of the whole story," Larissa told her. "You just need to be still and wait to see what the Lord has to say about this."

Tamara curled up on the couch and laid her head on Leah's shoulder. She wasn't ready for her sister and her sister-in-law to go back to Charlotte.

Leah wrapped her arm around her. "I wish we didn't have to leave you in a town where you don't have a single friend," she said, as if reading her mind.

"I do know someone here; I just haven't contacted her yet."

"That makes me feel a little better," Leah said.

"Yeah," Larissa put in. "At least you'll have someone nearby you can talk to when we're gone. Is she originally from Charlotte, too?"

Tamara shook her head. "We went to college together. She stole my first serious boyfriend and then married him."

"And you call this woman a friend?" Leah asked incredulously.

"I didn't say she was a good friend," Tamara admitted. "But she's changed since then. And so have I."

⟨⟩

"I really enjoyed the concert tonight," Savannah said, linking arms with Jonathan as they filed out of the arena and headed toward the parking lot. "Thanks for bringing me."

He smiled. "I had a great time, too. I get an extra boost of inspiration every time I see Tye Tribbett perform. I don't understand how that man can jump around as much as he does."

"Tye Tribbett was good, but it really wouldn't have mattered who was performing; I just enjoy spending time with you."

They reached the car, and Jonathan opened the passenger door for Savannah. "Do you really mean that?" he asked.

"Of course, I mean it. Why else would I have said it?" She gave him a frown of confusion. "You really don't know how special you are, do you?" With that, she ducked into the car.

He went around to the other side and sat behind the steering wheel. "I'm nothing special. Just a man with problems like any other."

She shook her head. "You made something of yourself, against all odds. Most women only dream of having a man like you in their lives. And the fact that you don't seem aware of that makes you even cuter." She gave his cheek a gentle pinch.

"I guess I'm just not used to receiving compliments from beautiful women."

"Well, get used to it. As long as we're dating, you're going to get plenty of compliments. And they'll be ones you deserve, not just empty flattery."

Smiling to himself as he pulled out of the parking lot, Jonathan wondered if he could get used to all the attention and affection Savannah lavished on him. It was a problem he didn't mind having, that was for sure.

"Are you free tomorrow night?" he asked her. "I think my ego could use some additional boosting, especially since I was just outbid on a contract I desperately wanted."

"Outbid, you say?" Savannah balled her fist like she was ready for a fight. "Tell me who it was, and I'll go give him a good punch in the nose."

Laughing, he put a hand over her fist. "No fighting. Anyway, I've already prayed about the situation. What God has for me is for me. So, if I'm meant to have it, the deal will come back around."

"See, that's what I don't understand about Christianity," Savannah said. "Friends of mine are always talking about what God has done or what He will do in their lives, as if they can't move unless this great invisible being instructs them whether to turn left or right."

"It's not like that," Jonathan responded patiently. "I just truly believe that God blesses His children. I am capable of doing many things on my own, if I so choose, but I like knowing that my heavenly Father has my back—that I don't have to do it alone."

Shaking her head, she said, "I guess, but I wasn't raised that way." She shifted her body so she was looking at him. "Don't get me wrong—my parents believed in the existence of a god, even though they didn't get up and go to church on Sunday mornings. But they were always preaching the survival of the fittest to me."

"My mother wasn't a regular churchgoer, either, but she made sure to take me on holidays like Christmas and Easter," Jonathan told her. "And at least once every other month we felt the need to be in the house of the Lord. But that was when I was a kid. Today, my mom is a dedicated Christian." He smiled as he added, "In fact, she was just ordained as a minister."

"That's funny. I thought Christians didn't believe women should preach."

The extent of Savannah's apparent ignorance about Christianity was a bit disturbing to Jonathan. Her remarks reminded him of the reason he'd never contacted her for a third date after the first two times they'd gone out. He knew in his heart that he would have nothing and be no one if God hadn't heard the pleas of a fatherless child. It had been

God who'd lifted up his head, and for that, Jonathan would be forever grateful. And any woman in his life needed to understand how essential the Lord was to existing and thriving.

After dropping Savannah off and returning home, Jonathan was feeling a bit bummed. His mood brightened, however, when he saw that his brother was still awake surfing channels in the living room. He plopped down on the other side of the sofa and propped his feet on the ottoman. "Thanks for waiting up for me."

Carter put down the remote and stared at him. "I wasn't waiting up for you. I do have a life, you know." He grinned. "How was your date?"

With a long-suffering sigh, Jonathan said, "It was going really good until I remembered why I stopped seeing Savannah in the first place."

Carter leaned forward. "Does this mean you're not going out with her anymore?"

Jonathan shook his head. "She's cool people. She just doesn't have faith in God, and that's a problem for me."

"Wow—my brother, dating an atheist?"

"I didn't say she was an atheist. She isn't against God, per se; she just doesn't believe that she needs to depend on Him. And I believe the exact opposite. So, unless she has a major change of heart, there's probably no use in continuing to date her." He pointed a finger at Carter and added, "I know you stayed up so you could grill me about my date. You ain't fooling nobody."

Carter waved his hand dismissively in the air. "Bro, I have plenty of things to do besides worry about your social life."

"Yeah, it sure looks like you have a lot going on, puttering around here waiting for the spring semester to start."

"I could get out of this condo and do some exploring…if I had a car," Carter told him with a sly grin.

He chuckled. "I'm not buying you a car. If you want something like that, you'll have to earn it." He was actually planning to surprise his brother with a car on the week he was scheduled to leave for college, but he saw nothing wrong with teaching him a life lesson in the meantime.

"How am I supposed to get a job when I don't have a car? It's not like there's a bus line within a mile of your condo."

"You could ride into work with me."

Carter perked up. "You're going to give me a job?"

"Why not? You're going to school for business management. I think it would be good for you to learn the family business from the ground up."

"So, on my summer breaks, I can come back here and work for you every year?" Carter asked excitedly. "I always thought I'd be stuck spending the summers flipping burgers in NOLA until I graduated."

Jonathan nodded. He'd been alone in this world for so long, he'd gotten used to the silence. But he didn't have to go it alone anymore. He had a brother, and he was going to do everything possible to help him.

Clearly playing cool, Carter bumped fists with Jonathan. "You're the best big brother a guy could have." He picked up the remote, leaned back against the sofa, and resumed flipping channels. "Now, if only my new job came with an office and a fat paycheck."

Jonathan picked up one of the sofa pillows and tossed it at him.

Ducking, Carter took the pillow from behind him and threw it back. Then he turned up the volume and pointed at the television. "Can you believe these guys?"

Jonathan turned his attention to the screen, but the show—like most TV programming—wasn't one he recognized. "What's this?"

"*Married at First Sight*. I just can't believe the men on this show were willing to marry a woman without knowing anything about her, or her mama, or the rest of her crazy family…nothing."

"They must have seen pictures of the women beforehand," Jonathan reasoned.

"Nope." Carter shook his head. "They go in blind. The one chick couldn't stand her husband for the first week of the experiment simply because she didn't like his looks once the blindfolds came off."

"How did these couples get hooked up if they didn't even know what each other looked like?" Jonathan hated to admit it, but he was intrigued.

"A panel of experts in psychology, sociology, spirituality, and the like match them up based on their compatibility. So far, it's looking like they did a pretty good job pairing off the couples. Except for that Vaughn guy—he complains about everything."

Jonathan couldn't help himself; he leaned back against the sofa and watched the rest of the episode. When it was over, he decided that the concept behind the show wasn't such a bad thing.

He'd never marry a woman he knew nothing about, but he liked the idea of knowing, from the moment he met a woman, that she was the one that the Lord had sent to be his bride.

When he headed to bed that night, Jonathan got down on his knees for a much-needed prayer. He'd tried and failed to pick a woman to spend the rest of his life with. Tamara didn't want him for anything but a friend, and Savannah thought he was a fool for putting his trust in God. Jonathan steepled his hands and prayed to his personal match-maker, "I need Your help, Lord. I'm tired of being alone, but, so far, I've done a terrible job of finding someone to spend my life with. Please help me to figure this thing out. Give me some type of sign, if that's what it takes, to point out my future wife. In Jesus' name, amen."

15

Tamara was in her dressing room, reading over the script for her segment of the weekend show. She'd thought that this new position would be so much more exciting than her career in Atlanta, but it was her second weekend on the job, and the excitement had yet to kick in. She didn't care about Jay-Z and Beyoncé's marriage or Nick Cannon's Twitter feed about his disintegrating relationship with Mariah Carey.

The only marriage she did care about was the one that might be happening between Jonathan and some woman named Savannah—someone he'd never even bothered mentioning to Tamara. She just wished he had been honest with her. And she wished he wouldn't have kissed her, because she hadn't been able to forget the warmth and the sense of being wanted, even if the act had meant nothing to him.

"Why can't I get him off my mind?" Frustrated, Tamara tossed her script down and paced the floor. She desperately needed to focus. Her boss had called her into his office after last weekend's segment and told her that it was evident that her mind wasn't on her job. "I need you to be a professional," he had said. "And perk up, for goodness' sake. Show us some of that cheerleading spirit."

She had been tempted to ask him if he was going to give the same pep talk to Greg Taylor, her forty-five-year-old male cohost. But she'd held her tongue and simply agreed to do better. Now, only minutes away from her next segment, she still couldn't get her head in the game.

Had she made the biggest mistake of her life by taking this job? In truth, Tamara had never imagined herself doing anything like this. Granted, her degree was in broadcast journalism, but she'd always envisioned herself working on something that helped advance the kingdom of God on earth. All this pop culture stuff was completely lost on her. For one, she didn't like to gossip and didn't believe in minding other people's business—not when there was so much of her own that she could be working on.

She wanted to scream. If she hadn't been so upset with her family and all their misdeeds, she probably wouldn't have pursued this position. And now she was stuck.

There was a knock on her door. "Five minutes," one of the assistants alerted her.

Tamara rushed back to her desk and picked up her script. She knew they were supposed to discuss the recent passing of two Hollywood icons, a few celebrity weddings, and an upcoming movie premier. It was nothing that determined the fate of the world or endeavored to help its citizens live a more fulfilled life, but it was the job she'd signed up for. She figured she had better do it to the best of her abilities.

Another knock sounded at her door. "Two minutes till airtime."

She put down the script, hoping that the teleprompter wasn't broken today. Standing up, she took a deep breath and walked out of her dressing room. Greg was standing by the anchor desk, looking not at all pleased with her. So far, they hadn't really developed a chemistry. It didn't help that he was the type of man who dyed his hair on the regular so that he could pretend to be ten years younger than he was.

"Why is your face all scrunched up, Greg?" Tamara asked in an exaggerated Southern drawl.

He scowled even more. "My face is 'all scrunched up,' as you put it, because I've been waiting for you to come out here and practice our segment for the last twenty minutes, but you never showed."

"I had no idea you were waiting on me."

"We agreed just last week to practice together. Don't you remember that conversation? Or has Alzheimer's taken up residence in your brain already?"

"I'm sorry that I forgot. But you could have knocked on my dressing room door to remind me."

"This isn't grade school, sweetie, and I'm not your father. I shouldn't have to remind you that there is work that needs to be done around here. You'd just better keep up, because I'm not slowing down the taping of this segment so you can try to figure things out."

There were so many things Tamara wanted to say, but none of them would have been nice, so she held her peace and turned away from Greg to allow the makeup artist to apply some powder underneath her eyes, covering up the bags that had started to form because of the sleepless nights she'd experienced since moving to Chicago.

"There. You're all beautiful again." The makeup artist grinned as she turned and retreated from the anchor desk.

Too bad Tamara didn't feel beautiful, smart, or "cheerleaderly" enough to get through this segment with Greg standing next to her. But in the next second, the cameras started rolling, and she had no choice. It was sink or swim.

She flashed the biggest smile she could muster. "Good afternoon, and thank you for tuning in to *This Weekend Live.*" Meanwhile, she doubted that very many people were tuned in. Not unless this channel was playing in all the shopping malls.

Greg took it from there, with Tamara chiming in as needed. The teleprompter was working as well as could be expected; it got stuck only twice, meaning that she lost her place no more than two times during the hour-long segment.

When the filming was over, she was relieved that she'd done pretty well, and Greg even had some words of affirmation. A genuine smile crept across her face as she began to believe that she just might be able to handle this job.

She went home and poured herself a bowl of cereal for dinner. After that, she ironed her dress for tomorrow's segment, then milled around the apartment until her eyes started to go crossed.

She opened her purse and took out the letter Belinda had written her. "You need a friend," she told herself.

She called the number that Belinda had included in the letter, then waited as it rang three times. She was about to hang up, feeling foolish for reaching out to a woman she hadn't had any type of friendship with in over a decade, but then Belinda picked up. She sounded so friendly that Tamara couldn't help but smile.

"Hey, Belinda. It's me, Tamara."

"Hi, Tamara! I was hoping that I would hear from you one of these days."

"I read your letter a while ago," she admitted, "but I recently moved to Chicago, and I was wondering if you might want to hang out or something, if you weren't busy."

"Tony has the kids this weekend, so I'm free. You want to grab a bite to eat?"

After a measly bowl of cereal, some real food sounded pretty good. "I could eat something, sure. Where would you like to meet?"

"If you just moved here, you don't know much about the area. Why don't you give me your address, and I'll pick you up?" Belinda suggested.

Tamara gave her the address and then threw on a pair of jeans, a T-shirt, and a sweater-vest. It took Belinda about forty minutes to reach her. When she got in the car, Belinda asked what she was in the mood for.

Tamara thought for a moment and surprised herself by saying, "I think I want a Chicago dog."

Belinda smiled. "I know the perfect place. It's not too far from here." It wasn't long before they reached Portillo's Hot Dogs. "This started out as a hot dog stand, but now they have locations all around Illinois, and even a few out of state."

"It's a fun atmosphere in here," Tamara commented as they made their way to the counter.

"Wait until you taste the hot dogs. Simply the best, bar none."

Sure enough, she had to admit that the hot dog was the best she'd had.

"I told you. Don't sleep on Portillo's."

"You sound like you were born and raised in the Midwest. But, if I remember correctly, your family is in South Carolina, right?"

Belinda nodded. "I came out here about seven years ago, when Tony was traded to the Bears. I wanted to divorce him before he switched teams, but he made me feel like it was my fault that he had to be traded— that if I had of kept my mouth shut and not allowed other people in our business, things would have been different. Yada, yada, yada."

Tamara shook her head. "He really tried to guilt-trip you into staying with him, huh?"

"You don't know the half of it." Belinda wiped her mouth with a napkin. "I was a fool for Tony back then. I put up with so much from him, just so I could be the wife of an NFL player. I just thank God that I think more of myself now."

"At least you woke up before it was too late and rebuilt your life into something you can be proud of."

"Yes, all thanks to the Lord, before whom I fall on my knees and pray to every night."

Tamara sighed. "I wish I could say the same. I haven't done much praying over the past few years."

"It's never too late to start," Belinda told her. "There must be something you're dealing with that you should turn over to the Lord in prayer."

Tamara brought her hand to her chest. "I would actually like for Him to help me understand how I allowed the allure of being with a baller to cost me the one man who truly loved me."

"Am I right in thinking that you're referring to Jonathan Hartman?" Blinking away tears, she nodded.

"I was surprised to see him with you at church. But then, I thought back to our college days and remembered how I used to think something was up between the two of you."

It seemed that everyone but Tamara had noticed her compatibility with Jonathan. And she knew the reason: She'd been too busy consuming herself with trying to marry someone who could make her an instant millionaire. She'd never concerned herself with how much heartache was likely to come with the man, the money, and the fame.

"Jonathan and I were just friends in college, but it turns out that he had strong feelings for me. I just didn't know it because I was too busy crying on his shoulder about Tony."

Belinda gave her a sympathetic smile. "Don't beat yourself up too much about it. We were cheerleaders back then. What else were we supposed to do but chase after the jocks?"

She managed a little giggle. "We could have tried studying a bit harder, for one thing."

"What would have been the fun in that?" Belinda stood up. "Come on. There's a secondhand shop near here where I like to shop, and I want to see if this gorgeous dress I've been eyeing for a while is still there."

Talk about a change of lifestyle. When she'd been married to a multimillionaire, Belinda had probably shopped at high-end boutiques— basically anywhere she saw fit—but she had been miserable. Today, she was racing to a secondhand shop, trying to get a good deal on a dress, and the smile that lit her face was priceless.

Back at her apartment later that night, Tamara determined that she wouldn't spend her life regretting things she'd done or hadn't done. She was tired of looking back on the disasters of yesterday. It was time for her to start enjoying every day of her life. With God's help, she would move forward.

Just before climbing under the covers, she knelt by her bedside to talk to her heavenly Father. "Lord God, I'm so thankful that You always hear me when I pray. I love You, Father, and I thank You for showing me that I still love my earthly father just as much as I always have."

She was surprised how natural it felt to pray, even after such a prolonged silence. She was just having a conversation, talking to God as she would to an old friend. Telling Him the secrets in her heart.

"I've been really sad for a long time now, Lord, but I'm tired of living this way. I've alienated myself from my family. And, to tell You the truth, I miss them more than I ever thought I would.

"I miss Jonathan, too, Lord. But if You desire for him to be with someone else, then please help me to stop thinking about him and wondering what might have been. I just want to live my life and enjoy whatever You help me to make of it." Taking a deep breath, she concluded, "Thank You, Lord Jesus. Thank You for the peace that You alone can bring."

She slept better that night than she had in months. When she awoke at dawn, she took a quick shower, then sat down to a breakfast of a grapefruit and some granola while watching a live broadcast of a pastor's sermon. It ended just in time for her to get dressed and head to the studio.

That day, she made sure to meet up with Greg to practice beforehand. He complimented her once during the run-through, and she decided that she would take what she could get from him. Smiling sweetly, she said, "Thank you, Greg. My goal is to do this job to the best of my ability. Any help I can get from you would be appreciated."

"You got it," he said, giving her a thumbs-up.

When the segment started, Tamara was all smiles—genuine this time—as she looked into the camera and said, "Good Sunday morning to you, and thanks once again for tuning in to *This Weekend Live*."

From that moment on, she knew that her star was on the rise with this station. She could not only do this job; she could excel at it.

When the cameras stopped rolling, Greg eyed her with surprise. "Whoa, what's gotten into you? It actually seemed like you were enjoying yourself."

She smiled. "To tell you the truth, all I did was pray. I've been really homesick, but I finally decided to stop letting that impair my performance on the job."

Greg shook her hand as if they were meeting for the first time. "Glad to have you here."

She left work that day feeling much better about her ability to contribute to her job and about her new life in Chicago. She hung out with Belinda again on Tuesday and also accepted an invitation to the mid-week service at Belinda's church. It was so nice to have a true friend.

"I really enjoyed the service," she told Belinda afterward, as the two were crossing the parking lot to their cars. "Thanks so much for inviting me. I needed to be here tonight."

"Yeah, and you heard what Pastor said—it's not over until Jesus calls us home."

"It was a powerful message," Tamara agreed.

"You know what I kept thinking after he said that?"

Tamara pulled her car keys out of her purse. "What?"

"That you should call Jonathan."

She stared at Belinda as if the woman were growing a second head. "What am I supposed to do? Call and say, 'When's the wedding?'"

"Now, what did we just hear Pastor say? It's not over…."

"I don't know, Belinda. That's not me. I could never scheme to steal a man from another woman, no matter how much I wanted him for myself." After saying those words, she clapped her hand over her mouth. "I'm so sorry. I didn't mean that the way it came out."

Belinda flicked her wrist. "I'm not offended. Stealing a man is wrong. I would never do something like that again, and I'm not suggesting that you do it, either. I just think you should call to see where his head is at."

"I'll think about it, but I'm not so sure it's a good idea."

"Why in the world not? Your article was just published, and several syndicated papers picked it up, as well. He could at least say thank you."

Tamara wanted to laugh at that notion. Belinda didn't know the whole story; she wasn't aware that Jonathan had been ambivalent about having the article printed in the first place. "I doubt he's ready to lavish praise on me. But if he wants to talk about the article, he has my number."

As she drove home, she dismissed all thoughts of Jonathan and his ladylove, not wanting to ruin the evening with self-torment. She popped a disc of praise music in her CD player and spent the remainder of the drive worshipping God and praying. "Thank You, Lord, for always being there for me. I love You so much, Father. Please help me to continue growing in You."

Likely thanks to her new outlook on life, the rest of her week went great. She was getting to know the city and finding comfort in her job. Not everything was the way she wanted it to be, but Tamara was determined to live with peace and joy as her constant companions.

On Saturday, one of the producers of *This Weekend Live* reported that the show's viewership had increased by 2 percent since Tamara's first weekend on the job. It wasn't a racial uptick, but it was enough to show that her presence was making a difference, and she was happy about that.

But on Sunday, the surpassing sense of peace and joy that Tamara had been experiencing was destroyed with a single phone call.

She had just put her bowl in the sink and was headed to her room to get dressed for work when her cell rang. It was Leah, so she picked up and said, "Why aren't you in church? I thought I was the only heathen in this family who had to work on Sunday mornings."

Leah didn't laugh at the joke. She took a deep breath and said, "I hate having to tell you this over the phone, Tamara, but Adam's been hurt."

Now Leah was crying. Tamara clutched the phone tighter. "What's wrong? What happened to Adam?"

"P-Portia tried to kill him," Leah stammered through her tears. "He's in intensive care, and…and it's all my fault."

16

Tamara's mind drifted back a few years to the last time that Adam had been in intensive care. Leah had blamed herself for that incident as well...

Tamara was seated on a couch in the hospital waiting room with Solomon and Larissa. Adam had just been shot and was being treated at the same hospital where her father had recuperated from a recent heart attack. Everybody was feeling pretty low, but Leah was the worst. She was hunched in a chair against the wall in a nearby alcove, her head down, her arms wrapped around herself. She looked like a child who'd been ordered to the corner for a time-out.

Solomon tilted his head at Leah. "Why is she sitting over there?" he asked Larissa.

Larissa leaned closer to him. "She blames herself," she whispered. "All of this started because she wanted to get even with her father, and now Adam is fighting for his life."

"That's a lot of weight for one person to hold on her shoulders."

"It is," Larissa agreed. "Why don't you go talk to her?"

"She's not interested in anything I have to say."

"Don't be like that." She nudged him out of his seat. "You might be the one God gives the right words to say."

Solomon scooted over to a chair by Leah. When she looked up at him with a question in her eyes, he said, "I thought you might want some company."

Leah scoffed. "Are you sure you want to do that? Being in company with me might get you exiled from this family."

Solomon chuckled. "I've already been exiled for most of my life, remember? I'm the half brother you knew nothing about until this year."

"Maybe you're right," Leah said with a sigh. "What else can they do to you besides take you out of the will? The truth is, Adam and I would love it if they did that." She sounded on the verge of sobbing as she added, "But who knows if Adam will outlive our parents? Maybe it will be his name that's taken out of the will."

"Don't do this to yourself, Leah," Solomon pleaded. "You've got to have faith. I believe that God is able to do the impossible. What about you?"

She shook her head. "I used to believe. Then again, I used to believe in Santa Claus and the Easter bunny, too. Shows how much I know."

"Adam needs you to be strong for him," Solomon told her. "He's in there fighting for his life, and he needs us to be praying and believing that God can bring him out of the nightmare he's in. Do you think you'd be willing to pray along with me, Larissa, and Tamara?"

Chewing her lip and twirling her hair around her finger, Leah said, "They don't want me messing up their prayers."

"I don't think you'd be 'messing up' anything. And I think Larissa and Tamara need just as much support as you do right now. I can see how much *you're hurting, and I know that you love your brother and wouldn't have wanted anything like this to happen to him."*

She unfolded her arms and turned to Solomon. "Why are you being so nice to me? I sure haven't been nice to you."

"We're family, right?"

Leah nodded without hesitation this time.

Solomon grabbed hold of her hand, helped her stand up, and led her over to Larissa and Tamara. "Do you two mind if we join you?" he asked them.

Tamara moved over and patted the seat next to her. "Take a load off."

"That's just what we need to do," Solomon said. "Would you two join hands with us as we pray for a speedy recovery for Adam? I think Leah would feel a lot better if we did that."

Larissa popped up from her chair. "Absolutely. I'd love to."

Tamara was a little slower to stand, but she soon clasped hands with Leah and Solomon. "We did a group prayer earlier with Mama and Daddy, but I guess I don't see the harm in praying again."

After they had prayed, Tamara opened her eyes and saw that tears were streaming down Leah's face. Larissa reached over and wiped her cheeks with a tissue. "We've done enough crying for today," she said. "Adam is going to be all right. Let's just keep praying for him."

Solomon had been there for Leah during her time of need, but Tamara was the one comforting her now. "Stop crying, Leah. This is not your fault. If Portia harmed Adam, then she is to blame."

"But Portia never would have been so jealous if I hadn't brought Carla and Britney back into Adam's life in the first place."

The sins we pay for. Tamara closed her eyes for a silent prayer that her family wouldn't continue to pay for this thing that Leah had set in motion after finding out about their father's secret son. It was time for their family to heal, once and for all.

"Let me pack a bag and book a flight. I'll be there as soon as I can."

The plane ride home was bittersweet. Tamara had been missing her family, especially when she'd been second-guessing her decision to take the job. That problem had since been solved, but when she called her boss to inform him that she wouldn't be able to tape that afternoon's show because she had to fly back home to deal with a family emergency, he not-so-politely suggested that she stay in Charlotte, and fired her on the spot.

The job had been growing on her, but if the network couldn't understand her need to be with her family at a time like this, then she was glad she'd been fired now, before she became too attached to the city and the people there.

Good thing her apartment had come furnished. She hadn't felt at home enough to put up any pictures, either, so all she had to do was retrieve the rest of her clothes and other belongings and move back home. Maybe Solomon would have some wisdom to offer on how to minimize the penalties for breaking her lease.

Right now, she just wanted to get to the hospital and make sure that Adam was all right. She still didn't understand how Portia could have inflicted intentional harm on the father of her children, but she'd known that her sister-in-law was pure evil from day one. Of course, no one had listened to her. Tamara only prayed that her father wouldn't suffer another heart attack over this incident. And maybe, just maybe, Adam would finally get enough guts to divorce Portia…if he lived.

Quit thinking like that, Tamara chastised herself. *Adam will live. He will be just fine.* She kept declaring those things to herself throughout the flight home. And she declared them out loud to Larissa when she picked her up at the airport. Normally, Leah would have come, but evidently she was too shaken by everything that had occurred that she was in no condition to drive her car or even to leave the hospital, for that matter.

⁓

After church on Sunday, with tickets to the Panthers game, Jonathan and Carter rushed home and loaded the cooler of water bottles and soda cans in the back of Carter's new SUV. Jonathan had ignored his brother's talks about wanting a Mustang, having had nightmares about his younger brother testing the speed and ending up with his car wrapped around a telephone pole.

He wanted him driving a vehicle that was solid and had some bulk to withstand impact, in case of an accident. So, he'd tried to take away the sting of not getting the longed-for Mustang by giving the eighteen-year-old a BMW SUV.

"Let's get this tailgating party started," Carter said as he climbed into the driver's seat.

Jonathan slid into the passenger seat. "I hope Solomon brings enough food. He was talking about fixing burgers and brats."

"I forgot the chips—be right back." Carter dashed back inside, then returned less than a minute later.

Halfway to the Bank of America Stadium, Jonathan's cell phone rang. It was Solomon, so he answered, "I hope you've got that grill going, because Carter and I are starving. We couldn't get out of church fast enough."

"I'm sorry, buddy, but I'm going to have to cancel on the tailgating," Solomon said, his voice filled with pain.

Jonathan switched the phone to his left ear. "Are you okay? You don't sound too good."

"It's my half brother, Adam. His wife ran him over with her car this morning, and he ended up in the hospital. We're there now, waiting on the doctors to let us know his prognosis. Larissa just went to the airport to pick up Tamara. There's just no way we'll be able to make the game today."

"I'm so sorry to hear that. Is there anything I can do?"

"You can send up a few prayers for Adam." Solomon's voice caught as he added, "And for my father."

"I'll do that. And I'll reach out to you later to see how everyone is doing," Jonathan said before ending the call.

When he explained the change of plans to Carter, the teenager gasped. "That's awful. Why would his own wife do something like that to him?"

"Who knows?"

"What about the game?" Carter asked, looking apprehensive.

"We'll still go. You've been looking forward to this game since you moved here. We can stop by Bojangles' on the way for some fried chicken and biscuits. I told Solomon that I would pray for them, and I intend to do exactly that while you drive us to the stadium, if you don't mind listening in on my conversation with the Lord."

"Okay, but don't forget to pray for Tamara, too. Adam is her brother, you know."

"Of course I'm going to pray for Tamara." Jonathan had given up his dream of a happily ever after with her, and the article she'd written just might ruin his career, but that didn't change the fact that he cared very deeply about her. So, as he prayed and asked God to be with Adam and to heal him, he also prayed that God would be with the entire Davison family and heal their hearts of their broken condition. Then he sent up a special prayer for the girl he'd known and loved for so long: "Lord, shower Your love on Tamara. Wherever she is right now, whatever she's doing, please wrap Your loving arms around her and let her know that she is special to You and that You care about what concerns her, in Jesus' name."

⌒

By the time Tamara reached the hospital, Adam was out of surgery but had yet to wake up. The rest of her family members were in the waiting room, along with Carla and Britney. Tamara rushed over to her parents and hugged them both. "I got here as soon as I could."

"We know you did, hon." Her mother kissed her on the cheek. "I'm just sorry you had to leave work for something like this. I'm sorry that it took a tragedy to bring you home."

"Well, it looks like I'm home for good, because I was just fired."

"What?" Her father shook his head. "That's ridiculous. You had a serious family emergency. And if they couldn't understand that, then who needs them?"

"That's just what I said, Daddy. What God has for me is for me, right?"

"Right, baby girl." There were tears in her father's eyes as he said, "I'm so glad to have you back home again."

"And I'm glad to be home." Tamara would have given almost anything to alter the circumstances that had brought her home, but that didn't change the fact that she was thankful to find herself surrounded by her family.

She looked around the waiting room for Leah and spotted her curled up in the same alcove where she'd sat the last time Adam had been in intensive care. Solomon was talking with Larissa, so Tamara decided to play the role of comforter this time. She crossed the room and stood behind her sister. "Hey, big sis. You got room for one more over here on the pity party side of the room?"

"What's your pity party about?" Leah asked without looking up.

"Let's see..." She sat down next to her sister. "My sister-in-law tried to murder my brother. My sister blames herself. And—oh, yeah. I got fired today."

Leah sat up and spun around in her seat. "You were fired for coming home to check on Adam?"

Tamara shook her head. "I think it had more to do with my having a rocky start on the job and then having the nerve to leave town without advance notice."

"Well, it's their loss."

"Not too much of a loss, but I appreciate your saying that, Sis." She leaned over and pulled Leah into an embrace. "Now, what about you?"

Leah wiped the tears from her eyes. "What about me?"

"When are you going to realize that God has forgiven you for what you tried to do to Daddy? Our entire family has forgiven you. When will you let go of the guilt you've put on yourself?"

"It sounds so simple when you say it."

"I realize it can be hard to believe it for yourself," Tamara said. "It's like how I understood the concept of forgiveness for everybody except my own father. I tried to punish Daddy by moving as far away as I could. But I ended up missing you all so much that the only person I really punished was myself."

"We missed you, too. And I'll take what you just said to heart."

"Please do, because Adam isn't back there fighting for his life because of anything you did." She pointed toward the double doors of the intensive care unit. "He's back there because of the woman the police arrested."

"Why didn't he divorce that woman?" Leah asked.

"I have no idea." Tamara leaned back against the wall. They would ride out this storm, spending the night at the hospital and praying that, by morning, Adam would somehow still be alive.

⟋

On Monday, Jonathan had an unprecedented experience in his career: He received a call about the job he'd initially lost because another company had outbid him. The bid had fallen apart because the guy hadn't been able to get financing, and now the city had to get rid of the land; and even though there'd been another bid even lower than Jonathan's, the commissioner rang him up.

"I'm a bit shocked by this call, Commissioner," Jonathan admitted. "I thought this deal was dead, because there were two bids lower than mine. If one of those deals fell through, I figured you would go with the other option."

"Price wasn't the only determining factor," the commissioner explained. "We want to partner with someone whose values reflect our Carolina ways. Your spirit of giving does just that, and it's something we want to be a part of."

Jonathan was so elated at getting the job that he had forgot to ask the commissioner what he meant by "your spirit of giving." They'd hung up before he could address the subject. "Oh, well." He lifted his water glass from his desk and made a toast to himself. "Here's to my spirit of giving." He swallowed a swig of water, then set down the glass, jumped out of his chair, and danced around his office, praising God with hands lifted high. He was so thankful to God for everything that He'd given him along the way.

Several minutes later, his door opened, and Jonathan spun around to see Carter rushing into his office. Adding his brother to the payroll had been a great idea. The boy was no slacker and wasn't afraid of a little hard work.

"Bro, should I call you Saint Jonathan or what?" Carter asked as he handed Jonathan a copy of the *Charlotte Observer*.

"How do you even know what's here?" Jonathan asked. "I've never even seen you as much as glance at a newspaper."

"I do a little more than just glance at a paper when my big brother is representing." Carter nodded at the publication. "Tamara made you look like some kind of angel sent down from heaven. I knew she was good people—I just knew it!"

"What are you talking about?" Sitting down, Jonathan opened the paper and began searching for the article Carter was referring to. He held his breath as he flipped the pages, wondering if it were possible that Tamara had written the piece in such a way as to show that she valued their friendship more than her chance to use her "gotcha!" question and make a name for herself.

"Flip back," Carter told him. "Page two."

Jonathan returned to the designated page. Sure enough, the headline read, "Commercial construction tycoon builds on a spirit of giving." Jonathan read the article in its entirety, his smile growing with every sentence. Not one word had been mentioned about the faulty wiring in the house he had remodeled all those years ago. Tamara's article cast him in the most positive light possible. In all honesty, he didn't deserve all her glowing comments. He did believe in giving back and doing good for others, but only because of all that God had done for him.

"I know I'm not supposed to mention Tamara's name," Carter said, "but the way she gushed all over you in that interview kind of seems like she's feeling you, Bro."

Jonathan grabbed his jacket off the back of his chair and stood. "There's someplace I need to be. I'll see you at home later this evening, okay?"

"Sure. Go handle your business," Carter said as he rushed out the door. "I won't be waiting up for you this time!" he hollered after him.

17

Tamara wrung her hands as she paced the floor of the intensive care unit. Following surgery, Adam had experienced some swelling in his head, so the doctors had put him in a medically induced coma to try to allow the swelling to go down without causing further harm.

"What does that mean?" Tamara had screamed at the doctors. "How can you just put someone in a coma? Will he ever come out?" She'd been truly shaken. Just last weekend, she had reported an update on a celebrity who'd been placed in a medically induced coma, only to die a few days later.

The doctors had tried to put her at ease, but she'd refused to be comforted. Finally, her mother had intervened and pulled her away from the doctors, thanking them for the update.

"I'm sorry, Mama," Tamara sobbed into her shoulder. "I just wanted to make sure they knew what they were doing."

"Of course." Her mother patted her back. "But your father and I have surrendered the situation to God. Adam's health is in His hands, so we need to leave the doctors alone and let them do their job."

She understood where her mother was coming from, but she was finding it especially hard to "let go and let God."

Just then, she remembered a praise song that she had listened to in her car after church the previous week. When she'd first heard "Let Go" by DeWayne Woods, she'd thought it was a nice song; but in the face of this current trial, the lyrics began to minister to her. She couldn't handle this situation on her own, so she needed to let go and let God.

All she could do now was call out to the One she had trusted since childhood. Leaving her family in the waiting room, she went to the hospital chapel to pray. Finding it empty, she sat in one of the pews and gazed up at the wooden cross that was suspended from the wall above the altar.

Tears welled in her eyes and began sliding down her cheeks. Her brother didn't deserve the pains and hardships he'd had to endure as a result of his marrying a woman who was not heaven-sent. He'd made mistakes, but he was a good guy. And even though Adam's errors, along with her father's, had caused Tamara to run in the opposite direction of her family, she couldn't imagine being anywhere else right now. Adam was a decent man who would give the shirt off his back to anyone in need…just like Jonathan. "Why is this happening?"

She got down on her knees, steepled her hands, and began pouring her heart out to the Lord. "Lord Jesus, I thank You for being so awesome in our lives. For You have truly blessed us and made us to walk uprightly before You. I don't know why Portia decided to harm Adam…I don't know if he was cheating on her with Carla, as she assumed…but I do know that Adam loves You and that he desires to be pleasing in Your sight."

Wrapping her arms around herself, she continued, "My brother is in a coma, Lord. And if You don't help us, I don't know what we're going to do. If Adam dies, my family will be devastated." The thought of the pain that Adam's death would cause her family sent a jolt through her body, and she began to weep as she tried to articulate the words that were in her heart. She was so overcome with sadness that all she could say was, "My faith is in You, Father. I brought all my cares in here so that I could cast them at Your feet. Receive my cares, Jesus, because I can't be consumed with worry and fear right now. I trust You to help Adam. Thank You, Lord. Amen."

She stayed on the floor, hoping to hear from God. But after about thirty minutes of hearing only the sound of her sobs, she dried her face with the hem of her shirt and stood up. She didn't know what the outcome of the situation would be, but she had prayed, and she trusted God to take care of the rest.

She headed back to the ICU, praying that Adam's condition had changed for the better since she had been gone. As she rounded the corner and started down the final stretch of hallway, she spotted Jonathan standing at the nurses' station.

When he saw her, he turned back to the nurse. "There she is," he told her, then returned his gaze to Tamara.

Jonathan hadn't returned any of her calls or made any comments about the draft of the interview that she had sent to him, but none of that mattered now. She didn't even care that he probably had a serious girlfriend. She was just so happy to see him in her time of need that she dismissed the memory of any rift that might be between them and ran into his arms.

⌣

"Jonathan...Jonathan...Jonathan." Tamara kept repeating his name as she clung to him. "I'm so glad you're here."

Jonathan felt like the worst kind of jerk for going to the game last night with Carter instead of coming to the hospital. Tamara had needed him, and he hadn't been there for her. He closed his eyes as a sharp pain pierced his heart. Then, for the briefest moment, the earth seemed to shake beneath his feet. But they were in North Carolina, not California, so it couldn't have been a tremor.

"Are you all right?" she asked, stepping back.

"It's just…I can't explain." Nor did he want to explain what he was feeling at that moment. Because, as he looked into her eyes, he knew that God was telling him she was the one. Tamara Davison was the closest thing to heaven he was ever going to find on God's green earth, but he doubted she was ready to know what was in his heart. And he hadn't come to the hospital to pour out his feelings to her. He'd come to be a friend. "I wanted to be here with you. I should have been here yesterday, but I was being a bonehead."

"Can we do each other a favor and not dwell on what we did or didn't do for each other in the past? I'm just happy to have you here with me." She looped her arm in his, and they headed toward the ICU waiting room to rejoin the rest of her family.

⌒

Tamara went straight to her family, huddled in the back of the waiting room. "What's going on?" she asked. "Any news?"

"Not yet," her father said, then stepped aside and shook Jonathan's hand. "Thank you for coming out here. Tamara could really use a friend right now."

"That's why I'm here, sir."

"You're a good man, Jonathan," Tamara's mother said while staring pointedly at her daughter.

Before Tamara could respond, Carla reentered the waiting room. She'd been there all night with Britney but had left early in the morning to work her shift at Burger King.

Britney ran to greet her mother. "I didn't think you were coming back today."

"I'm on my lunch break and I thought I should clear the air," Carla said, then bit down on her lip.

"No one here blames you for what happened to Adam," Solomon told her.

"I know, but he was run down in front of my house, and I just wanted to make sure you all knew that Adam and I weren't carrying on like Portia thought. He was at the house to help Britney study for her college exams." Tears flowed down Carla's face as she added, "I never got very far in school. I guess I didn't apply myself like I should have. That's why I've been stuck in one low-wage job after another. But Britney is smart."

"Of course, she's smart—she's a Davison, isn't she?" Tamara's father said.

Smiling, Carla finished by saying, "I just want her to succeed. And Adam wanted...wants that, too. Portia was just blinded by resentment. She called me last week and told me that she wouldn't give up a dime for Britney to go to college. I guess she just lost her mind when she realized that Adam was helping his daughter with something that might cost them some money."

"It always comes back to money with Portia," Leah said. "I just thank God that she is behind bars, where she belongs."

"You and me both," Tamara's mother admitted. "The kids are at her parents' house, but Adam will want to see them when he..." Her voice broke for a moment, but she cleared her throat and said, "When he wakes up."

Tamara's father put a hand on his wife's shoulder to calm her. "He's going to wake up, Alma." Then he looked around at each person gathered with them. "I expect you all to believe that. There's no place for doubters here."

Everyone nodded, and several responded, "We believe."

"All right, then." The bishop put one arm around his wife and the other around Britney. "I think it's time that we go to God in prayer and make our requests known, because my son is coming out of this coma today." His words carried unusual force and conviction.

No one argued or hesitated. They all joined hands and bombarded heaven with prayers for Adam. They prayed so fervently that Tamara imagined Adam could hear them, even though he was separated by a set of thick doors, not to mention still in a coma.

⁓

After the final "amen," Jonathan took Tamara down to the cafeteria to grab a bite to eat.

"Are you sure you can take the day off like this?" Tamara asked him. "Don't you have work to do?"

"More than you can imagine." He smiled, thinking about the contract he'd just won. "But the work will keep. I rarely take time off, so today, I'm going to just hang out with you and not even think about whatever work may be piling up back at the office."

But he was having a hard time not thinking about the contract he'd just won, especially since his victory had been due to her decision to highlight opportunities he had taken to give rather than take from others. It was as if she had heard what his heart had been trying to say that day he'd spilled his guts about his first nightmare house flip.

As they sat at the cafeteria table eating their sandwiches, Jonathan couldn't keep it in any longer. "I was surprised by what you wrote in that article."

"You wouldn't have been if you had read the draft my editor sent to you over a month ago."

With his head down, he admitted, "I sent it back without opening it. I didn't want to read about my greatest failure."

"You're the one who said it was okay to write about your first project," Tamara pointed out.

"I know. But I find it interesting that even though you wrote about the fire and how it led to the hiring of my foreman, Hank, you never mentioned that I feared that the fire might have been my fault due to the faulty wiring."

Tamara shrugged one shoulder. "You did a generous thing by hiring that man. The world didn't need to know anything else, especially since it wasn't faulty wiring that caused the house fire in the first place."

"Hank did a generous thing by giving me a clear glimpse of God at work in all the madness I was going through at that time. He's the real hero, not me."

"The fact that you don't see yourself as a hero for all the good works you've done through the years just makes you that much more of a hero in my book," Tamara told him.

Jonathan reached out and touched her hand. "Thank you for being a friend. You could have exposed me to the world and potentially ruined the future growth of my company. But instead, your article helped me land a contract I had previously lost to another bidder."

Beaming from ear to ear, she put her free hand on top of his. "Happy to be of service. Maybe you can give me another interview once I find a job down here."

Leaning back, he freed his hand from hers. "Uh, no to the interview. But can you repeat what you just said? Am I to understand that you're no longer in Chicago?"

"They fired me."

"Tamara, I'm so sorry to hear that."

She waved him off. "It was for the best. I didn't like being so far away from my family. When I heard what had happened to Adam, I told my boss that I was taking the next flight home, and he basically told me not to come back."

"Well, it's their loss, you know."

Laughing, she told him, "They didn't lose much. I was doing a terrible job. I think I was too homesick to focus. But I was getting better. Each segment we filmed was an improvement from the previous one, and the show's viewership had gone up by two percent since my arrival."

Jonathan was relieved to see that she didn't seem too devastated over the job loss. "Just let me know if there's anything I can do to help with your job search. I can certainly provide a reference—I'll vouch that you're a wonderful interviewer who always paints her subjects in a far more positive light than they deserve." He grinned.

Shaking her head, Tamara told him, "Keep your endorsements to yourself. It's my job to elicit those unexpected comments—the details that turn the interview on its head. I can't promise that every person I interview will be pleased with the end result."

Becoming serious again, he simply said, "I do appreciate what you did for me."

"And I appreciate your being here with me right now. You don't know how awful I've been feeling. You've even made me laugh a few times."

"That's what I'm here for. Ladies laugh at me all the time."

"I'm sure they don't." Tamara took a bite of her sandwich and studied him with a thoughtful expression on her face. She took a sip of her iced tea, then said, "I'm sure Savannah doesn't laugh at you."

His heart stuttered for a moment, and he raised his eyebrows. "You know Savannah?"

She shook her head. "I've never met her; I've just heard how serious you are about her." Plastering on a smile he recognized as fake, she added, "I think it's great. I'm so glad that you finally found someone. Just make sure I get an invitation to the wedding."

Narrowing his eyes now, he asked her, "Was it Carter who told you about Savannah?"

Tamara nodded. "He wasn't trying to rat you out or anything. He simply explained that you had received my voicemail message but were out on a date with your girlfriend."

Jonathan shook his head. "I don't know why Carter would exaggerate the situation, unless he was trying to make you jealous. The truth is, Savannah is not my girlfriend. Yes, I took her out on a few dates, but she and I are not spiritually compatible. And so, I remain single, as always."

"Why would Carter want me to be jealous?" she asked.

He decided not to tiptoe around the issue. "He knows how I felt about you in college, and he has it in his head that we should be together."

"And what about now, Jonathan? Do you still feel the same way about me? Or have your feelings changed?" Tamara appeared shocked at her own boldness, but she watched him with an expectant look on her face, as if her curiosity in knowing the answer exceeded her embarrassment in posing the question.

Jonathan stared at her for a long moment, trying to decide how to respond. Before he could say anything, however, Tamara's cell phone chirped, alerting her that she'd received a text message.

She looked at her phone and read the message on the screen, then jumped out of her seat, frantic. "Adam just had a seizure."

18

Tamara sat with her family as they waited to hear exactly what was going on. Fear was evident on every face. Seizures were bad news, and even Larissa, herself a doctor, looked more worried than ever. But Tamara wasn't ready to give up, as everyone else seemed prepared to do. "I don't like the way everyone is acting," she announced. "I didn't come back home just to bury my brother. We need to do something about this."

"What are we supposed to do?" Leah asked, wiping the tears from her eyes. "Adam isn't doing well at all. I mean, come on—let's be real. Seizures are never a good sign."

Their father stood, towering over his family, a determined expression on his face. "Tamara is right. We can't just sit here, waiting on the doctors to come out and pronounce my son a vegetable or, worse yet, dead. Adam will live and declare the goodness of our Lord, and that's all there is to it." He held out his hands. "The only thing I know to do, whether life is easy or hard, is to pray, pray, and then pray some more."

Tamara's mother stood up and joined hands with her husband. "I'm with you, David. We can't just sit around and worry. Not when we know God like we do."

Tamara and Jonathan, seated next to each other, got to their feet and clasped hands as the whole group bowed their heads in prayer for Adam. And in the moment when their hands touched, Tamara got a glimpse of what forever would feel like with this man. She had known him for so long—had considered him a friend for most of that time—and she couldn't understand how she'd been such a fool as to miss seeing Jonathan for who he was way back in the beginning. She saw now that Jonathan was the total package: handsome, successful, and caring.

Back then, she had been too busy chasing after ballers, because she'd thought cheerleaders were meant to be with athletes. Now, she realized that former cheerleaders were meant to be happy, by picking the right person to spend the rest of their lives with.

Her brother had been a baller in high school and college. He'd married a cheerleader, and look where that had gotten him.

"Lord Jesus, we come to You, lifting You up and giving You all the glory for what You are about to do in Adam's life." Her father's voice was powerful and booming as he called on the Lord, believing that every word he uttered would be heard.

As her father continued praying, Tamara smiled. This was the father she knew—a man of committed faith who was dedicated to his family. Bishop David Davison was a good man—not perfect, but good. She wished she had never doubted him, either. She was doing a lot of second-guessing about the men in her life these days. But this time, without a shadow of doubt, she knew that she was viewing him in the right light.

"Father God, Adam is in Your capable hands," her father continued. "We don't accept all that is going on around us. We have decided not to look to the left or to the right but always up to You. Lead us and guide us, because we are lost sheep without You.

"Healing is in the blood, and we ask that the blood of Jesus run through Adam's body and heal him right now. My son won't die from this, but he will be healed and restored to even better health than he had before the devil tried to steal his life. No weapon formed against him shall prosper. That's what your Word says, and I believe it."

"I believe it, too," Tamara responded.

"Me, too," Larissa declared.

One by one, every person made a declaration of faith in the goodness of the Lord. Several other people in the waiting room joined in, and pretty soon, someone was playing praise songs on his cell phone while Tamara, her mother, Leah, and Larissa were dancing down the aisles of chairs. The Davison family had decided not to go down without a Holy Ghost fight. They weren't going to stop praising God until He descended on them.

After about an hour of the Davisons lifting holy hands and praising the Lord in the waiting room as if they were in church on a Sunday morning, the double doors to the ICU opened, and Dr. Peters rushed out. There was a smile on his face as he approached Tamara's parents. Clasping a clipboard, he told them, "The swelling has gone down, and your son hasn't had any additional seizures."

Tamara's mother pumped her fist in the air. "Praise God! Is he awake? Can we see him?"

Dr. Peters shook his head. "We haven't brought him out of the coma yet. I want to give him a few more hours. This thing is not an exact science, but I don't want to pull him out too soon."

"You do what you have to do, Dr. Peters, because my son is coming out of this coma, and he is going to live," she proclaimed for all to hear.

"Yes, ma'am. I'll do my best." With that, Dr. Peters pivoted on his heel and went back through the doors to the ICU.

Bishop Davison turned to his family. "We can see that God has already started moving on Adam's behalf. The swelling has gone down, and the next step will be to bring him out of his induced coma. So, I need y'all to grab a spot, get down on your knees, and pray until something happens."

Leah retreated to a corner by herself; Larissa and Solomon selected a couch on which to sit and pray; Tamara's parents joined hands and got down on their knees, facing each other, and continued calling on the Lord, asking Him to have mercy on Adam.

Tamara and Jonathan moved to a spot in the back of the waiting room. Before getting on her knees, Tamara told Jonathan, "You don't have to do this. I appreciate your coming here today, but my family will pull an all-nighter praying for Adam, if we have to. I don't expect you to hang with us that long."

"I'll be here all night, if that's how long it takes."

"Are you sure, Jonathan? What about Carter?"

He pulled his cell phone out of his jacket pocket. "Let me text him and tell him to grab a pizza or something for dinner."

"But he's going to be alone."

"Carter is a big boy. He'll understand." Jonathan sent the text, then turned off his phone off and returned it to his pocket. He reached out for her hands. "Should we get down on our knees or just stand here and pray?"

Tears were pooling in Tamara's eyes. Never in her life had any man offered so much of himself to her without expecting anything in return. She knew then, without a shadow of a doubt, that she loved Jonathan Hartman. She only wished that she'd had the good sense to realize it back in college.

"Let's get down on our knees, okay?"

Without another word, he lowered himself to the floor, pulled Tamara down beside him, and began calling on the matchless name of the Lord.

Tamara echoed his prayer in her heart, but before long, her mind drifted back to her college years, to the day that the spiraling events of her life were set in motion.

It was homecoming weekend of her junior year, and Tamara was on the football field, cheering her heart out with the other cheerleaders. She was having a tough time of it, though, because the cheerleader standing right next to her—one who'd pretended to be her friend—had just stolen her boyfriend.

She'd been nursing a broken heart all week, and Jonathan had been there for her the whole time. He'd comforted her, and she'd appreciated every minute spent with him. More than once over the course of the week, Tamara had wondered to herself if she was supposed to be with a guy like Jonathan rather than the jocks who normally chased her around campus.

But then, the night before the big game, the team quarterback, Mike Barnes, had approached her. He'd said that he heard she was now single and that he wanted to let her know how special she was. Mike had even gone so far as to kiss her on the cheek before walking away.

She was supposed to meet up with Jonathan after the game to hang out and grab a pizza. But when the game was over, Mike was so excited about winning that he ran over to Tamara, picked her up, and kissed her on the mouth.

Jokingly, Tamara had then called him her hero. As Mike set her back down on the ground, she glanced around and saw Jonathan walking away, looking devastated and defeated. She started toward him, wanting to explain.

But Mike grabbed her arm. "Where do you think you're going?"

"I see a friend over there I need to talk to."

Shaking his head, Mike told her, "Not tonight, baby. Tonight, we're going to celebrate, because this is only the beginning. This win will help propel me into the NFL, and I'm planning to take you with me."

"Me?" She couldn't believe Mike thought that much of her. After all, they'd been together only a day.

"Who else? You're the best catch on the campus, and I aim to keep you with me from here on out."

"Here on out" had lasted three months until Mike had found the next best thing on campus. Tamara had been left heartbroken once again, but this time, Jonathan hadn't been there to pick up the pieces. He had transferred to another school, and Tamara had been so wrapped up in all the hype around Mike Barnes that she hadn't stopped to consider that perhaps it had been her interactions with Mike after the homecoming game that had prompted Jonathan's desire to attend a different school.

Tamara's mind drifted back to the present, and she realized that Jonathan was still praying for Adam. She also noticed the tears streaming down her face. But these tears weren't only for Adam—they were also for the foolish girl she had been so many years ago. How she had stood back and let Jonathan walk out of her life, she couldn't explain; but even as she prayed for Adam, she also asked God that He would show her how to keep Jonathan around for good this time.

19

It worked! As the Bible said, the prayers of a righteous man avail much. Adam had come out of his coma. He was a little groggy, but other than that, he seemed fine. "If you were trying to get this family to start praying together again, you accomplished that," Leah told him jokingly.

"I could feel your prayers," Adam said, serious. "I can't explain it, but it was like a stirring in my soul."

The room went silent as the group pondered Adam's statement. Tamara understood what he was saying, because she had felt a stirring in her soul the more they had praised and prayed to God on her brother's behalf.

"That just goes to show that Daddy knew what he was talking about when he would tell us to kneel down and pray about our problems, because God was willing and able to help us with whatever concerned us," she finally said.

"It's funny you remembered that just now," Larissa told her, "because I was thinking about how Uncle David used to say that to us, even before we could understand what he was talking about."

Tamara smiled at her, then turned to her brother. "The doctor said we could come in for only a minute, and Daddy and Mama made us promise not to tire you out. So, we'll head back to the waiting room with them so that Britney can come in for a short visit."

Before she could move, Adam reached out and took hold of her arm. "Where is Portia?"

With a sharp intake of breath at the mention of that woman's name at a time like this, Tamara told him, "She's in jail. Last I heard, her arraignment was scheduled for tomorrow."

Adam nodded, then looked at Larissa. "Tell Solomon I need to see him."

The next day, Tamara still wanted to ask: Were they being punked? Had the induced coma caused Adam to lose his mind? She was flat-out confused by the turn of events that had unfolded since he had awakened. Because now, every member of the family except Adam—and their mother, who refused to leave her son's bedside—was preparing to enter in courtroom B, where they would watch Solomon defend yet another woman accused of harming their beloved brother.

But this time, Solomon was representing the accused at the victim's request. And they were all in court at Adam's behest.

When they filed into the courtroom, Tamara's father leading the procession, Tamara noticed that Portia's parents were already seated on the bench directly behind the defense's table. Tamara wanted to sit behind the prosecution. She might be here at her brother's request, but Portia needed to be prosecuted, no doubt about that. She just didn't understand why Adam wanted to help her. Maybe the high-dosage pain medication was to blame. Once Adam came down off whatever they had him on, he would release Solomon from Portia's case and allow her to be tried, found guilty, and sentenced to the punishment she justly deserved.

Bishop Davison went straight to the bench behind the defense's table to greet Portia's parents. As he did, Tamara whispered in Leah's ear, "For goodness' sake, let's just be human today and treat these people the way our flesh wants to."

"You know how Daddy is," Leah told her. "He lives out his faith at all times, whether in the pulpit or not."

They watched as their father hugged Maria and Larry Lewis and told them, "We came to support Portia. Adam didn't want her to go through this without all her family here."

"I notice that your wife isn't here," Maria remarked.

"Alma's at the hospital with our boy, so the rest of us came here to be with our girl," the bishop replied without a trace of malice in his tone.

"Thank you for saying that," Larry put in. "We don't know what's going on between Portia and Adam, but I know it will do her heart good to see you all here to support her."

Maria harrumphed. "Don't you be thanking him so soon. Alma is probably at that hospital plotting against our baby."

"Calm down, Maria. These people have been family to Portia for seventeen years. They aren't our enemy," Larry said, trying to talk some sense into his wife. But she just harrumphed again as she turned up her nose at the Davison family.

Solomon took his place at the defense's table.

"What's he doing?" Maria hissed. "I thought Portia was being represented by a public defender."

Larissa leaned forward in her seat. "Adam asked Solomon to help Portia," she explained quietly.

"Oh, he'll help her, all right—help her into a life sentence." Then the woman turned on her husband. "Why didn't you give Portia some money for an attorney? Do you want to see her in prison?"

Her husband bowed his head. "I didn't have the money for an attorney, Maria. You know that."

"All rise," said the bailiff.

As everyone stood, the judge got into position, and then Portia was led into the courtroom. She looked like she had spent the night in a coma herself. Her hair was going in all directions, and her eyes were wild, spilling tears with every step. When she looked at Solomon and then spotted all her family—her parents and the Davisons—she broke down and had to be helped to her seat.

The judge had no patience for the waterworks. He began the hearing and asked Portia how she pleaded.

Portia couldn't respond. All she could do was moan and shake her head.

Solomon looked to the judge. "Please excuse my client. She is overcome with grief."

"I can see that," the judge said. "But for the purposes of this hearing, I need to know how you're going to plead this case."

Clearing his throat, Solomon stood up straight and adjusted his tie. "Not guilty, by reason of insanity. Your Honor, I'd like to request a psychological evaluation of my client."

Maria jumped out of her seat. "My daughter's not crazy! What kind of help is this? I want a new lawyer. I demand a new lawyer!"

The judge banged the gavel as Larry pulled his wife back down to her seat. "Quiet in the courtroom," the judge barked. "Any more outbursts, and I'll have my bailiff escort you from the court. Is that clear?"

Maria folded her arms over her chest in a display of defiance, but she didn't open her mouth again. The judge then turned back to Solomon and said, "I'll order a psychological evaluation. We will set the trial date once the evaluation is complete."

The prosecutor spoke up next. "We can wait on the results before going to trial, Your Honor; but, due to the viciousness of this crime, I'm requesting that the defendant be held without bail."

"Your Honor," Solomon protested, "my client is a wife and mother who has—"

"She might be a wife, but she came this close"—the prosecutor held his thumb and index finger less than an inch apart—"to being a widow, and because of her own doing. So, for the safety of her husband and their children, I don't think this woman should be released. At least, not until her mental state has been examined."

"I'm inclined to agree with you on that." The gavel came down. "No bail."

As the bailiff escorted Portia from the room, she looked around as if she didn't know where she was. "What's going on? Where's my husband? Where're my kids?" She tried pulling away from the bailiff. "I want to go home. Mama!" she screamed. "Tell them that I want to go home."

"Okay, baby, I'll tell them." Maria walked behind her daughter for a moment. Then she grabbed hold of Portia and tried to pull her out of the bailiff's grip. Other bailiffs had to be called to assist, and soon both Portia and Maria were hauled off to the county jail.

Larry stayed behind a moment. When the commotion died down, he shook hands with Solomon and then with Tamara's father. "Thank you for what you're doing for my daughter. I just hope these doctors can figure out what's wrong with her."

"So, you see it, too?" Solomon asked. "Adam says that the woman we see now is nothing like the woman he married. He thinks that she has some sort of mental condition. He also thinks it might be hereditary."

Shoulders slumping, Larry nodded. "I see it. I've seen the same instability in her mother for a long time, but I've never known what to do, other than whatever's necessary to keep the peace."

David put a hand on Larry's shoulder. "Maybe now we can get them both some help."

With a sigh that conveyed decades of frustration, Larry said, "Let me go see if I can bail Maria out."

"I've always thought Adam was some kind of saint for enduring Portia's antics for this long," Tamara told her father. "But if she's dealing with some sort of mental illness, then I really feel bad that I never tried to reach out to her."

"None of us knew anything was wrong with Portia," Larissa put in. "A lot of people are able to mask mental conditions until something happens that causes them to snap. And it looks like Portia has finally reached that point."

There was sadness in Leah's eyes as she said, "I feel at least partially responsible for Portia's breakdown. If I hadn't brought Carla and Britney into the picture, then maybe she wouldn't have gone all crazy. Maybe her condition could have stayed under wraps, and the rest of us would have gone on thinking that Portia had a problem but not knowing she was mentally ill."

"You can't blame yourself for this, Leah," their father said. "Our family needed to know that Britney was out there. We love her, and I'm very happy to have her as my granddaughter."

"I know that, Daddy, but I didn't bring Britney's existence to light because I thought you would appreciate having another grandchild. I was being vindictive, plain and simple. But I'm letting all of you know, right here and right now, that I don't have a vindictive bone in my body anymore. I have seen the damage that comes from trying to hurt another person in the name of revenge, and I'm truly sorry."

Their father hugged Leah. When they pulled apart, he wiped away the tears that were running down her face. "You've already been forgiven, daughter. Now I need you to forgive yourself."

"I'm working on it, Daddy," she assured him. "I'm getting there."

"Well, you need to work a little harder," Tamara told her as she wrapped her in an embrace. "Because we don't blame you for any part of what transpired between Portia and Adam."

"And now it seems like we can't totally blame Portia, either—not if she's legitimately ill," Larissa said.

Tamara was still grappling with that one. After what she had witnessed today, she could believe that Portia had some kind of mental illness. And, based on her mother's behavior, Tamara would be willing to bet that the illness was indeed hereditary.

At that thought, she was reminded of the inheritance that her mother and father had set up for their children. Because the Davisons had lived well, theirs was, above all, a spiritual inheritance. And Tamara would take that over the biggest financial inheritance in the world.

The following week, as the family sat around Adam's hospital room, waiting for the nurse to return with the paperwork okaying his release, Adam thanked Solomon for representing Portia in court.

"Don't give it another thought," Solomon told him. "I'm just glad that I was able to help out on this one."

"I can't help but give it thought, Solomon. I treated you terribly when Dad first told us about you. But you're my brother, and I am thankful that God planted you in this family, because you have been the glue that's kept us all together."

Solomon smiled at that. "Mrs. Lewis sure wasn't thankful for me. She still won't accept the results of Portia's evaluation. But I think that's because she needs an evaluation herself. I sure hope that Mr. Lewis orders one for her…and before she takes a baseball bat to my head, like she threatened to do."

"Welcome to my world, Brother," Adam said, giving rise to a chorus of laughter. It had a nervous quality to it, though, because they finally knew what they were dealing with.

The results of Portia's psychological evaluation had come back with the diagnosis of a paranoid personality disorder. Tamara had done a Google search to find out more about the disorder, and as she read the description of the average individual with paranoia—"hard to get along with," "struggles with close relationships," "may alternate between acting excessively suspicious or hostile and aloof or withdrawn," "often acts guarded or 'cold'"—it felt as if the words had been written by someone who personally knew Portia.

All these years, she'd wondered why Portia was so hard to get along with, and she'd just assumed the woman was alternately aloof and hostile in a strategy to control the situation. But now she knew that Portia needed help, especially after the therapist had informed them that Portia's disorder had blossomed into full-blown schizophrenia. The one good thing about the entire episode was that Portia was finally able to get the medication and treatment she needed to get better.

"It seems strange to say," Leah began, "but I don't think any of us were surprised at the diagnosis Portia received. We were never able to treat her like a true member of our family because she always seemed so suspicious, like she thought we were plotting against her. I never understood it until now."

Adam nodded. "I just want my kids to know that none of this would have happened if their mother hadn't been ill." He looked at Solomon. "I'm grateful that you were able to get the evaluation done."

"I think Portia wanted the evaluation as much as you did," Solomon told him. "After coming to grips with what she'd done to you, she was an emotional wreck. But when I saw her yesterday, she seemed at peace."

"I just hope that none of our kids inherits the disorder," Adam said quietly.

"That's what you have family for," Tamara told him. "We are going to keep those kids covered with the blood of Jesus, and we'll help you watch out for them."

"We sure will," their mother assured him. "With the God we serve, I can guarantee you that my grandchildren will be just fine."

"What are your plans for when Portia gets out of the hospital?" Leah asked him. "Do you think you'll get back together with her?"

Solomon had delivered the results of Portia's evaluation to the prosecutor that very morning. The prosecutor had looked them over and agreed that she should be allowed to plead not guilty by reason of mental defect. If the judge signed off, Portia would be placed in a mental hospital until she could demonstrate that she was no longer a danger to herself or anyone else.

Adam shook his head. "I honestly don't know. I still love my wife, and I want to help her. So, I won't leave her while she is in the hospital. I hope you all can understand that." They nodded as he continued, "My job right now is to cover my wife and all my children. I'm going to pray about what the future holds for Portia and me, but, most of all, I'm going to pray for her total healing from this disorder."

Although Tamara would worry for her brother's safety if he decided to stay married to Portia, his unwavering love for her brought hope to her heart—hope that Jonathan's love for her might have endured for all these years.

20

In the parking lot outside Bank of America Stadium, Solomon lowered the tailgate of his truck and pulled out the grill. Once it had heated up, Jonathan threw on the marinated steaks and chicken legs. Tamara and Leah set up the card table and unloaded the folding chairs from the trunk, while Larissa and Carter got to work assembling a salad and some sandwiches from the veggies and cold cuts stashed in the cooler.

While the tailgaters next to them were gulping down cans of Bud Light and blasting country music, Leah turned their radio to Praise 92.7 and started passing out bottles of water and soda. *Christians have just as much fun as everyone else,* Jonathan thought, *they just don't have the headaches later.*

Across the parking lot, a man wearing a Panthers jersey raised his beer in the air and started dancing around, moving from truck to truck and hollering, "Get live! Get live!"

"He's certainly live right now," Larissa observed. "Hopefully, he won't throw up out here. Vomit is the last thing I want to smell today." She scrunched her nose and rubbed her belly.

"You and me both," Tamara agreed. "I've seen enough drunk fans to last me a lifetime."

They enjoyed one another's company and a tasty meal for two hours or so, until it was time to head into the stadium for the Panthers game.

Jonathan put an arm around Tamara as they made their way to their seats. It felt right to be this way with her, like she was his and he was hers. When Tamara smiled up at him, for the first time since meeting her, Jonathan actually believed that the gleam in her eye was directed at him—and him alone. Could it be true? He wanted to kiss her right then and there, but there were too many people around. He'd purchased the tickets online, and their seats were right near the fifty-yard line, well in view of all the cameras, too.

The game got off to a great start, the Panthers taking no prisoners, so the stadium was rowdy. Fans leaped out of their seats as the quarterback ran the ball; they hooted and hollered when he threw for a touchdown.

Jonathan was having the time of his life. He'd been to one game already, with Carter and with Savannah; but today was a day like no other, because Tamara was with him, and she was smiling at him as if he meant something to her.

During the third quarter, Tamara leaned over. "I need something to drink."

"What do you want? I'm happy to get it." Jonathan started to stand, only too willing to be her errand boy.

She stood with him. "You don't have to do that. I need to stretch my legs, anyway."

"Then I'll come with you." He stepped aside to let her out of the row, then followed her up the stairs to the promenade. They walked arm in arm to the nearest concession stand, where Tamara ordered a lemonade and Jonathan purchased a bottle of water.

Tamara put her arm around his waist as they made their way back to their seats, getting him grinning like a high schooler who had just scored a date with the captain of the cheerleading squad. Yet Tamara was so much more than some trophy on his arm or a notch in his belt. She was the woman he wanted to spend the rest of his life with. He decided then and there that he would talk to her about his feelings as he drove her home that night.

They were just a few steps from their seats when a huge guy bumped into Tamara. Jonathan pulled her back, trying to give the man enough room to go around them.

"So sorry," he said over his shoulder. "I wasn't paying attention. Too busy watching the game."

"Don't give it another thought," Tamara told him. "I'm fine."

As if the sound of her voice had jarred him, the guy turned his entire body around to face her. Eyes wide, he said, "Tamara?"

"In the flesh."

Finally, Jonathan recognized the man. It was Mike Barnes, the college football player who'd gone pro and played in the NFL for seven years before back problems had forced him out of the game. Now he was a highly successful sports commentator.

"Mike? Wow, it's been a while. How have you been?" Tamara asked.

Jonathan didn't like the way she was smiling at Mike Barnes. This was the same guy who'd swooped in the last time he'd been about to pour out his heart to her and had stolen her away from him.

"We should get back to our seats," he told Tamara.

But she only put a hand on his arm. "You remember Mike, don't you? He was quarterback of the college football team."

"I remember him," Jonathan said, extending his hand to the man. "How've you been?"

"Real good, real good." The expression on Mike's face made it clear that he didn't recognize or remember Jonathan.

"Mike, you may not remember Jonathan Hartman—he transferred to a different school shortly after the start of junior year. He's a builder/real estate developer here in Charlotte and a close friend of mine."

"Well, any friend of Tamara's is a friend of mine," Mike said with a grin.

"I'm going to go sit down," Jonathan told Tamara. He was tired of the chitchat.

"Okay. I'll meet you there in a minute. I just want to catch up with Mike."

Jonathan was fuming as he left the two of them alone. Too bad their seats weren't out of earshot. He could hear their conversation loud and clear.

"I've seen you on ESPN," Tamara told Mike. "You're doing a great job over there."

"Retirement wasn't for me. I had to do something else. And why not do it around the game that I love so much?"

"I'm glad you found something that you enjoy doing, even if you're not on the field anymore."

She sounded truly happy for him. Considering the way he'd dumped her back in college, Jonathan just didn't understand. Was she looking for a repeat with the man? Did she think he had changed his ways?

"It was nice seeing you, Mike, but I should get back to my seat."

"How about lunch or dinner? I'm in town for a few more days."

"Give me your card. I'll call and try to work out a time for us to meet for lunch before you leave."

Tamara rushed back to her seat, but she could tell that something had changed between her and Jonathan within the brief span of time it had taken them to get their drinks and get back to their seats. He no longer looked as if he was enjoying the game—or being with her, for that matter.

As the clock wound down to the final seconds, she leaned closer to him. "Are you okay?"

"I'm fine," he snapped. "Why wouldn't I be?"

She didn't know how to respond to that. He was acting as if she'd wronged him in some way, but she couldn't figure out what she'd done to him.

As they got up from their seats, Mike Barnes waved from the promenade. "Nice seeing you again, Tamara. Don't forget to call."

"I won't," she assured him, waving back.

"Do you want him to give you a ride home?" Jonathan asked her. "Because if you do, it's fine with me."

She stumbled backward as if she'd been slapped. Larissa came up behind her—she and Solomon had been seated several rows over—and reached out to break her fall. "What did you have in that cup?" she teased. "Have you been drinking like the party-man at the tailgate?"

She and Solomon were laughing, but as far as Tamara was concerned, there wasn't an ounce of humor in what Jonathan had just said to her. "No, I haven't been drinking. But I'm going to need a ride home."

"I thought you were riding with Jonathan," Leah said as they began their trek up the bleachers.

"I was, but now I think Jonathan must have something else to do. He just asked me to find another way home."

Jonathan pulled Tamara to the side. Keeping his voice low, he said, "That's not what I meant, and you know it. If you're not riding with Mike, I can take you home."

She narrowed her eyes as she freed her arm from his grasp. "I'm not riding with Mike, and I'm not riding with you, either. Good night, Jonathan. It's been a real experience." Then she turned back to her sister. "You ready?"

"Um…I was going to—Yeah, I guess I'm ready," Leah finally said as she dug inside her purse for her keys, her eyes clouded with confusion.

Tamara linked arms with Leah. "Good. Let's go."

In the privacy of the car, Leah turned to her. "Okay, what's going on? Why aren't you riding with Jonathan?"

"Just drive, please."

Leah put the key in the ignition and started the car. As she pulled into the line of cars waiting to leave the parking lot, Tamara covered her face with her hands and started crying.

"Hey! What happened back there?"

"Why do I fall in love with jerks?" Tamara blurted out. Tears were flowing down her face as she shook her head. "I think I had it right when I said I didn't want to date at all."

"But the only reason you said that was because of what you'd learned about Daddy and Adam. I think you need to realize that men can be faithful and loyal. Just look at how loyal Adam is being to Portia. And that woman doesn't deserve his loyalty at all."

"I g-guess you're right," Tamara stammered. She took a series of deep breaths, trying to avoid breaking into all-out hysterics. "I was wrong to judge Daddy and Adam so harshly, and to assume that all men are like them. And I was finally getting over that, thinking that Jonathan might be the one. But I don't want to be with any man who acts the way he just did."

"Jonathan seems like a great guy, Tamara. Don't you think you might be overreacting just a little? I can't imagine him doing anything to hurt you on purpose."

"Well, he did, and that's a wrap for me. I'm just going to concentrate on finding a job and forget about men and love and all that happily-ever-after nonsense."

Tamara was still crying when they arrived at her parents' house. After parking in the driveway, Leah called their mother and asked that she come outside and help her get Tamara inside.

When their mother reached the car and saw Tamara crying, she yanked open the passenger door. "What's wrong with her?" she demanded of Leah as she reached in to pull her younger daughter out.

"She got in an argument with Jonathan."

Tamara was still crying like a baby who'd just had her favorite toy taken away from her.

"Must have been some argument. I've never seen her like this."

Leaning on her mother, Tamara stumbled along the walkway to the front door, Leah trailing behind them.

Tamara's father opened the screen door wide and enfolded her in a hug. "After the storm we just came through with Adam, I doubt anything can be as bad as this seems."

"She had a fight with Jonathan," Leah told him.

"Is that all?" he asked as he led Tamara into the family room.

"Is that all?" She wriggled free from his embrace and gawked at him. "I just came to terms with the fact that I love Jonathan, and was believing that God intended for us to be together…and now it's over. Before it even began."

"How is that possible?" her mother asked, rubbing Tamara's back to comfort her.

Taking a deep breath, she willed herself to stop crying. She wiped the remaining tears from her eyes. "I won't be with a man who thinks so little of me that he…that he…. Oh, just forget it. It's over, and that's it." She left the room without saying anything else, but she didn't make it far, slumping into a chair in the hallway to continue her crying.

"What do you think?" she heard her mother ask her father. "Can it really be over already, when they had finally found each other again?"

"Tamara can be really stubborn," her father responded, "so I just don't know."

"Are you kidding me?" Leah scoffed. "You two may be exhausted from all the praying you did for Adam, but I'm not about to let you give up on Tamara and Jonathan. He is perfect for her. So, I say that we do as Daddy always taught us: Pray until Jonathan's heart is moved to get him over here and make things right with Tamara."

"Spoken like a true Davison," her father said.

Tamara couldn't resist peeking around the corner. She watched as her father extended one hand to his wife and the other to Leah. "Shall we?"

"Let's," her mother agreed. "We've just witnessed how awesome God is and how mightily and swiftly He can change situations and circumstances. Now we'll petition him on Tamara's behalf."

Tamara was deeply moved as her father began praying. "Our Father, who is the God of heaven and earth, we come to You now, lifting up Tamara and Jonathan. You know all, You see all, and You can fix all. Our faith is not moved by Tamara's declarations, because our faith is in You. Work this thing out for them, Lord. If You desire for them to be together, then open their eyes…"

21

You messed up, Bro. Tamara looked like she wanted to hurt you bad," Carter said as he entered the condo after the game.

Jonathan made no move to get up from the couch, where he'd been moping for the past half hour. "I don't want to talk about it."

"You don't need to talk about it with me. You need to go to Tamara and talk to her about whatever it is that's bothering you."

Carter's precocious wisdom was lost on Jonathan at the moment. All he wanted to do was sit there and mourn the love he had lost not once but twice in his lifetime. Tamara's agreeing to call Mike Barnes, while he stood right there with them, was the ultimate slap in the face. He couldn't simply brush it aside and pretend it hadn't happened.

Carter sat down across from him and just waited.

Jonathan didn't know what to think or do. He was devastated by Tamara's actions, and it was beginning to dawn on him that he was still carrying around the hurt he'd experienced back in college. Back when Tamara had called Mike Barnes her hero.

Jonathan looked up at his brother. With Carter starting college in the next few months, he felt obligated to warn him about the dangers he would soon face. "Don't get too close to any woman when you get to college. Take my advice and focus on your studies."

"Whoa, man. I've never heard you sound so bitter before. You're always encouraging me to be positive about life."

"I'm still positive," Jonathan said. "I'm positive that you will get your heart broken if you fall in love with a woman who is interested solely in flashy guys."

Carter laughed at that. Pointing at Jonathan, he said, "Who's got more flash than you, Bro? I mean, give yourself some credit. You came from nothing and created a business empire, and you did it all without needing to know how to throw a ball or carry one without getting tackled. You made it with this." Carter tapped himself on the side of the head. "And I want to be flashy just like you."

"Being around Tamara and Mike Barnes today took me back to a time when I didn't have much and felt inferior to just about everybody."

"Well, you're not inferior to anyone," Carter told him. "You're my big brother, and you caused things to happen, man. You've got to know that you're important."

His words of affirmation caused Jonathan's chest to puff out a bit. He stood up and grabbed his keys. "You are so right, little brother. I don't have to take a backseat to anybody. And I'm going to let Ms. Tamara Davison know it, too."

"That's right!" Carter jumped up and yelled as if he were still at the football game. "You go get your woman."

Jonathan didn't know if he was going to come back with a victory, but this time, he wouldn't tuck tail and run away, like he'd done back in college. It was time for Tamara to figure out what she wanted. Either she wanted to be on his team, or she didn't. Simple as that.

But, being as he was a blood-bought child of the Most High God, he determined not to waste another minute worrying about it. What God had for him was for him. And he was about to find out whether Tamara was for him.

Jonathan didn't remember that Adam was recuperating at Tamara's parents' house until he pulled into the driveway. He was a little hesitant about going inside, because the last thing he wanted to do was cause this family any more stress than they were already experiencing. Now that he thought about it, he felt awful for the way he had treated Tamara at the game. She and her siblings deserved to do something fun after the harrowing reality they'd just endured, and he'd allowed his jealousy to ruin her chance to unwind.

He started to back out of the driveway, but the front door opened, and Leah ran out across the lawn toward him.

He parked the car and climbed out.

"Hey, stranger!" Leah greeted him. "I thought we might see you before the night was over."

"Why is that?" he asked, trying to sound nonchalant.

"Let's just say that I'm a praying woman, and you are the answer to the prayer I prayed tonight."

He wished he could be the answer to Tamara's prayers. "Actually, I was thinking of coming back another time. I know your family is dealing with a lot right now, so I figured I should probably just wait to talk things over with Tamara."

"Don't be silly. She's in there moping around. Your timing couldn't be better. Maybe you can put a smile back on her face."

He didn't know if he would be able to make her smile—not with what he'd come here to say. But he was grateful that he wasn't the only one dealing with misery tonight, as bad as that seemed. "I did drive all the way over here, so I guess the least I can do is say hello to everyone."

"Of course. And I'd like to introduce you to my brother Adam. He needs to know that you were right there with us, praying for his recovery."

Jonathan followed Leah into the house. Bishop Davison and Alma were watching TV in the family room. They looked up as Jonathan stepped inside.

"Good to see you, Jonathan," Bishop Davison said. "Did you have a good time at the game?"

"I did, sir. It's always a good time when you're with the right people."

"I'm glad you all enjoyed yourselves," Alma said. "Adam would have loved to have gone with you, but it was important for him to take advantage of the peace and quiet and get some rest." She was smiling from ear to ear as she discussed her son's progress. "He'll be back to normal in no time."

"God is good," Jonathan said, nodding his head.

"All the time," Bishop Davison put in.

"Come on," Leah said, pulling Jonathan down a hall toward the back of the house. "Let's go say a quick hello to Adam."

"Do you think it's okay to disturb him? I think your mom wants him to rest."

"We won't be in there long." Soon they reached a closed door. Leah knocked, waited a few seconds, and then pushed it open. "Adam? There's somebody here who wants to say hello."

Jonathan followed her into the room. That's when he noticed Tamara, seated next to Adam's bed.

Ignoring Tamara, Leah said to Adam, "I thought you might want to thank Jonathan. He came to the hospital and helped us pray you out of there."

"I certainly would like to thank him." Adam nodded at him. "Thanks for praying for me, man. As I told my family when I finally came to, I could feel the prayers."

"I'm just glad I was able to help in some small way."

"Ain't nothin' small about prayer," Adam told him with a grin.

Jonathan nodded. "You're right about that," he said, remembering all the prayers he'd sent heavenward as a child, begging God to do something miraculous in his life. God had listened back then, so he decided to send up one more quick prayer, in hopes that God wasn't finished taking care of what concerned him.

"What brings you over here tonight, Mr. Hartman?" Tamara asked, acknowledging Jonathan for the first time.

He could hear the ice in her voice. "I came to see you," he told her honestly.

"Sorry, but my dance card is all filled up. I guess you might as well go on back home."

"I deserve that," he acknowledged. "But I'm here, anyway, and I'd like to talk to you." He held his breath, silently praying that Tamara wouldn't ask him to leave.

"Is something going on that I should know about?" Adam asked, his eyes moving from Tamara to Jonathan.

"Nothing that you need to worry about." Tamara stood up. "You just relax and heal up. I'll be back in a few minutes to make sure you're still resting, like Mama said you should."

"Okay, warden." Adam chuckled.

Tamara pointed at him. "And no laughing, either."

"I'll watch him, don't worry," Leah said as Tamara filed out the door after Jonathan.

In the hallway, he wasn't sure which way to go, so he let Tamara take the lead. He followed her outside to the back patio, where she turned around, folded her arms in front of her chest, and glared at him.

"Look, I know I messed up, Tamara. But can you at least hear me out?"

She pursed her lips and moved her hands to her hips, but she still didn't say a word.

"I was jealous, okay? I shouldn't have acted the way I did, but it felt like being back in college again, watching Mike Barnes sweep you off your feet—your *hero*, as you called him."

Recognition registered on her face, and her expression softened. She dropped her hands to her sides. "You never gave me a chance to explain. Suddenly, you were gone, and we weren't friends anymore."

"I shouldn't have left so abruptly," Jonathan conceded, "but I just couldn't hang around and watch you fall for another football player, especially when I knew you were just going to end up getting your heart broken again. As much as I love you, I refuse to pick up the pieces one more time."

Tamara bit her lip. "Mike did his best to break my heart, but, to be truthful, it hurt more when I realized that you had transferred to a different school and wouldn't be coming back."

Letting his guard down all the way, he said, "It hurt when you agreed to go out with him while I was standing right there."

"I didn't agree to go out with Mike. I told him I'd consider meeting him for lunch."

He shoved his hands in his pockets and lowered his head. "Like I said, I was jealous, and I overreacted."

"You sure did. Especially if you thought I was the least bit interested in Mike Barnes."

His head popped up. "You mean you're not interested in him?"

"No, goofball." She laughed. "The guy dogged me back in college, and right now, he's on his third marriage, still paying alimony and child support to his two ex-wives. That's why he couldn't just retire from football without getting another gig. And the only reason I would've met up with him would have been because of his role at ESPN. You seem to forget that I'm in need of a job. Nothing wrong with a little networking, right?" She put her hands back on her hips. "Anyway, I can't believe you actually thought I was still that same shallow girl from college who would rather have a playboy over a real man."

Pulling his hands out of his pockets, Jonathan took a step toward Tamara. "I hope that the 'real man' you're referring to is me. Because I came over here to let you know that I'm in love with you."

Her eyes brightened. "You love me?"

He moved within mere inches of her. "I've been in love with you since the first week we met. I was too shy back then, and I didn't think that I had my life in order enough to tell you my true feelings. But I'm here now. I'm standing right here, with my heart in my hands, hoping and praying that I'm not in this alone."

Tamara reached out and pulled him closer. She opened his hands and placed hers in them. "I don't know why it took me so long to recognize just how important you are too me, but I'm here now, too, saying that you aren't in this alone." Her voice broke as tears filled her eyes. "I love you so much, Jonathan."

Joy filled his heart as he leaned down and tenderly kissed his lady-love. She kissed him right back, and when they finally came up for air, Jonathan hugged her to him. "I'll make you happy, Tamara, I promise you that."

"You've already made me happier than I ever thought I could be. I just can't believe I get to be in love with my best friend."

"Finally!" Leah shouted as she and her parents stormed the back patio.

Tamara whipped around. "Were you all spying on us?"

"We had to," Alma told her. "We needed to make sure you didn't mess this up again."

Tamara's hands went back to her hips. "Mama!"

"Lower those eyebrows and close that mouth, dear. You don't want to run Jonathan off. He just got here."

22

From that moment, it was on and popping between Tamara and Jonathan. They spent every spare minute together, just as they had in their early years of college. But Tamara wasn't the same college cheerleader in need of a superstar athlete to make her feel important. She now needed and desired the man God had put in her path.

Her short stint in Chicago had aided in landing her a new job as the host of *Charlotte Live*. On the show, Tamara highlighted pieces of news that would uplift and edify her viewers. She figured that if they wanted the gruesome and despicable details of celebrity scandals, they could turn on the regular news or just go online. But Tamara finally felt as if she were journeying toward her God-given purpose, and that made her happy.

This weekend, she would be moving into an apartment she'd found. As much as she loved her parents' house and felt more at home there than anyplace else, she needed to feel grown-up again, and that meant getting a place of her own.

After finishing her last interview for the day, she picked up her office phone to call Jonathan. A smile crossed her face the moment he answered. "Hey, you. I couldn't wait a moment longer to hear the sound of your voice."

"I was just sitting here thinking about you, too," he told her. "It's a wonder we get any work done."

Tamara laughed. "I'm a professional multitasker. I can work and think about the love of my life at the same time."

"Well, that's good for you. I'm about to call it quits for the day, because now that I'm talking to you, I know I won't be able to accomplish anything else until tomorrow."

"Is Carter excited to start college?"

"He is—and he's been driving me crazy," Jonathan said. "Are you still up for making the trip?"

"You bet! I wouldn't miss something so important to Carter. I even dusted off my pom-poms."

Jonathan groaned. "Will those really be necessary?"

"Don't be a big baby," Tamara chided him. "Carter needs cheering on every now and then, just like you do."

"Oh, all right. I know he'll appreciate your coming along to help with the move, anyway."

"You haven't forgotten our plans for Sunday afternoon, have you?"

"Nope. I'll be at your beck and call all day, unpacking as many boxes as you need me to."

"I love you, Jonathan Hartman."

"And I love you, Tamara Davison. See you in a little while."

"I wish I didn't have to leave today. I really want to be here to see Tamara's face when you pop the big question," Carter said.

"Well, I'm sorry, Bro, but that's just the way it is. Besides, I want the proposal to be private. Intimate." Jonathan pointed toward Carter's room. "Grab your bags so we can get on the road."

"Are you sure you have everything taken care of?"

Rolling his eyes, Jonathan said, "Boy, get your bags. I told you, Leah is taking care of things for me while I drive you to school. But if you'd rather catch the bus, I can get you a Greyhound ticket."

"No, no. That's all right. Besides, Tamara promised to cheer for me on the drive to school."

Jonathan playfully grabbed his brother by the collar. "Don't try to steal my woman."

Prying Jonathan's hands off his shirt, Carter told him, "If it wasn't for me, you wouldn't even have a woman. You are so lame when it comes to romance."

"Whatever," Jonathan muttered.

But as Carter rushed off to get his bags, he realized the kid was right about him. He had been lame. But he had seriously upped his game since he and Tamara had committed themselves to each other. Too bad Carter wouldn't get to witness just how much he'd improved. Maybe he'd send him some pictures after the big event.

⌒

During the drive to Chapel Hill, true to her word, Tamara sat in the front passenger seat with her pom-poms lifted, chanting as many cheers as she could remember from high school and college, making sure to adapt them to Carter as much as possible.

In between chants, Carter said, "You promise to come to visit, right?"

"Ooh, it sounds like somebody is getting homesick, even before he's all the way out the door," Tamara teased.

"I'm not homesick. Jonathan was a terrible roommate. Anyone I end up rooming with at college has to be better than my grouchy brother."

"You never know—I might still be feeling grouchy when the college okays you to bring your car to campus. Guess you'd better not count on me to drive it down here for you." Jonathan grinned at Carter in the rearview mirror.

"Did I say 'grouchy'?" Carter rushed to say. "I mix up my words sometimes. I really meant to say that he's been a wonderful roommate, and I'm really going to miss hanging out with him."

"I bet you'll get your car now," Tamara said, laughing hysterically.

Their good-natured banter continued for the rest of the ride. Tamara held Jonathan's hand during the last half hour; even though he wouldn't admit it, she knew that leaving Carter at school was going to hurt. She just wanted him to know that he wasn't alone. Not as long as she was by his side.

But once Carter had unpacked his bags in his dorm room, she was surprised by his apparent eagerness to rush them off the campus, and even more by the fact that Jonathan didn't seem to mind.

As they drove back to Charlotte, Tamara found herself staring at him, trying to figure out the situation.

"So, I guess I don't get any cheers from you, huh?" Jonathan asked.

"Actually, I'm a bit stunned," she told him. "I thought you'd have a hard time saying good-bye to Carter. And I thought he would want us to hang out with him for a little while. But neither of you seemed to care all that much."

"Oh, I'm going to miss Carter. But he'll have people his own age to hang out with at UNC. So, I can't fault him for being ready to get to it."

"If you say so," she answered, but she wasn't buying his explanation.

Once they arrived back in Charlotte, Jonathan took an unexpected turn into a luxury lake community called The Sanctuary, tucked away on a corner of Lake Wylie. Tamara had always loved this area, but the million-dollar houses had always been well out of range, so she'd never even considered looking at them.

"You know someone who lives over here?" she asked.

"I sure do," Jonathan said with a sneaky grin on his face. "Do you mind visiting with me?"

"Are you kidding? I would love to see the inside of one of these homes."

Several minutes later, Jonathan pulled the car into the driveway of a huge brick home. Tamara's mouth was practically hanging open. "You do business with someone who lives *here*?"

He unfastened his seat belt. "Come on. Let's go in and see."

She climbed out of the car and followed him up the three stone steps leading to the most magnificent porch she'd ever seen, complete with a hanging swing. She pulled out her cell phone and took a picture.

Jonathan chuckled. "What'd you do that for?"

"One day, I'm going to have a porch like this, and I want to remember what they did so that I can decorate mine the same way."

She turned and saw him grasp the front doorknob, then turn it.

"What are you doing?" she whispered. "You can't just walk into someone's house without knocking."

"You think the owners might call the police on us?"

"They might. Or they could just shoot you. People do things like that, you know."

"We're not going to get shot, I guarantee you that."

Tamara hesitated. "I don't know if I trust you on this one. Close that door and knock first."

"Okay." Jonathan closed the door again and then knocked—once, twice, three times. But no one came to the door.

"Were the residents expecting you?"

"They should have been." Jonathan opened the door again, ignoring Tamara's quiet protests, and strode inside. Standing in the foyer, he shouted, "Anybody home?"

No one answered. Tamara was still on the porch. He turned to her and said, "I thought you wanted to see the inside of one of these houses. Come on in."

She shook her head. "I'll just sit out here on the porch and wait for the owners to come home."

"Have it your way."

Just as she lowered herself into the porch swing, he came back out-side, fumbling with something in his jacket pocket.

Tamara turned her head and glanced through the front window. She couldn't believe her eyes. There, stacked in the living room, were a bunch of her boxes, ready to be moved to her new apartment.

She jumped out of her seat. "What's going on?" she demanded. "Why is my stuff in that room?"

"Give me a second, and I'll tell you."

Tamara rushed past Jonathan and into the house to get a closer look. Surely, she was mistaken about those boxes being hers. But, sure enough, they were filled with her belongings. And not only that, but the walls had been hung with the family photos she'd long kept in storage.

Jonathan came up behind her, and she turned to him, full of ques-tions. "You...you put my family photos on the walls."

"Actually, Leah did that for me. She told me that you refused to hang those pictures anywhere but a place that felt like home." As he said those words, Jonathan got on one knee and held out an open ring box. "I bought this house because I wanted you to have a place to call home. Now, I'm praying that you will want to make that home with me. Will you marry me, Tamara?"

With tears flowing down her face, she quickly nodded, then gave him a resounding "Yes."

Jonathan stood once more, slid the sparkling ring on Tamara's finger, and leaned in for a kiss.

Later that evening, as they shared a picnic dinner in the family room, surrounded by photos of some of the people she loved most, she told him, "Thank you for buying this house. No place has ever felt more like home to me."

"The house is all right, but being with you, with you here and right now, feels like heaven."

"Heaven on earth," Tamara corrected him. "And there's no place I'd rather be."

About the Author

Vanessa Miller is a best-selling author, playwright, and motivational speaker. Her stage productions include *Get You Some Business*, *Don't Turn Your Back on God*, and *Can't You Hear Them Crying*.

Vanessa has been writing since she was a young child. When she wasn't writing poetry, short stories, stage plays, and novels, reading great books consumed her free time. However, it wasn't until she committed her life to the Lord in 1994 that she realized all gifts and anointing come from God. She then set out to write redemption stories that glorified God.

Heaven on Earth follows *Feels like Heaven* in Vanessa's third series with Whitaker House. Her previous series are Morrison Family Secrets, comprising *Heirs of Rebellion* and *The Preacher, the Politician, and the Playboy*, and Second Chance at Love, of which the first book, *Yesterday's Promise*, was number one on the Black Christian Book Club national best-sellers list in April 2010. It was followed by *A Love for Tomorrow* and *A Promise of Forever Love*. In addition, Vanessa has published two other series, Forsaken and Rain, as well as a stand-alone title, *Long Time Coming*. Her books have received positive reviews, won Best Christian Fiction Awards, and topped best-sellers lists, including *Essence*. Vanessa is the recipient of numerous awards, including the Best Christian Fiction Mahogany Award 2003 and the Red Rose Award for Excellence in Christian Fiction 2004, and she was nominated for the NAACP Image Award (Christian Fiction) 2004.

Vanessa is a dedicated Christian and a devoted mother. She graduated from Capital University in Columbus, Ohio, with a degree in organizational communication. In 2007, Vanessa was ordained by her church as an exhorter. Vanessa believes this was the right position for her because God has called her to exhort readers and to help them rediscover their places with the Lord.

Welcome to Our House!

We Have a Special Gift for You ...

It is our privilege and pleasure to share in your love of Christian fiction by publishing books that enrich your life and encourage your faith.

To show our appreciation, we invite you to sign up to receive a specially selected **Reader Appreciation Gift**, with our compliments. Just go to the Web address at the bottom of this page.

God bless you as you seek a deeper walk with Him!

WE HAVE A GIFT FOR YOU. VISIT:

whpub.me/fictionthx

WHITAKER
HOUSE